The LOTTERYS Plus One

EMMA DONOGHUE

illustrated by
CAROLINE HADILAKSONO

ARTHUR A. LEVINE BOOKS
An Imprint of Scholastic Inc.

Library of Congress Cataloging-in-Publication Data

Names: Donoghue, Emma, 1969– author.
Title: The Lotterys plus one / Emma Donoghue.
Description: First edition. | New York : Arthur A. Levine Books, an imprint of
Scholastic Inc., 2017. | Summary: Once upon a time, two couples with Jamaican,
Mohawk, Indian, and Scottish ethnic roots won the lottery and bought a big house
where all of them, four adults and seven adopted and biological children, could live
together in harmony—but change is inevitable, especially when a disagreeable
grandfather comes to stay.
Identifiers: LCCN 2016008863 | ISBN 9780545925815 (hardcover : alk. paper)
Subjects: LCSH: Families—Ontario—Toronto—Juvenile fiction. | Brothers and
sisters—Juvenile fiction. | Grandfathers—Juvenile fiction. | Toronto (Ont.)—Juvenile
fiction. | CYAC: Family life—Fiction. | Brothers and sisters—Fiction. | Grandfathers—
Fiction. | Toronto (Ont.)—Fiction. | Canada—Fiction.
Classification: LCC PZ7.1.D66 Lo 2017 | DDC
823.914 [Fic]—dc23
LC record available at https://lccn.loc.gov/2016008863

10 9 8 7 6 5 4 3 2 1   17 18 19 20 21
Printed in the U.S.A.   110

First edition, April 2017

Book design by Abby Dening & Elizabeth B. Parisi

THE LOTTERYS PLUS ONE
IS DEDICATED TO MY MOTHER,
FRANCES PATRICIA RUTLEDGE DONOGHUE,
WITH LOVE AND THANKS
FOR ALL THE CONVERSATIONS.

Once upon a time, a man from Delhi and a man from Yukon fell in love, and so did a woman from Jamaica and a Mohawk woman. The two couples became best friends and had a baby together. When they won the lottery, they gave up their jobs and found a big old house where their family could learn and grow . . . and grow some more.

Now Sumac Lottery (age nine) is the fifth of seven kids, all named after trees. With their four parents and five pets, they fit perfectly in the Toronto home they call Camelottery.

But the one thing in life that never changes . . . is that sooner or later things change.

MaxiMum

CardaMom

FREE SHROOS

Wood

Catalpa

Sic

CHAPTER 1

THE DORMANT GRANDFATHER

O nly eight people at breakfast today, which feels weird. (Sumac's three eldest sibs have stayed on at Camp Jagged Falls for a wilderness trip.) But she has been quite enjoying the extra space. Even though Camelottery has thirty-two rooms, you'd be surprised how often all the Lotterys seem to wind up trying to use the same toilet at the same time.

Right now, Sumac's putting blueberries on her oatmeal in the Mess — which is Lottery-speak for their yellow-walled kitchen, because a mess is the place armies eat — and no one's jogged her elbow yet: amazing. She's made sure to be on the window side of the long table, facing the same way as her sister Aspen, who bobs up and down on her

I

exercise ball so much that if Sumac sits across from her she feels seasick. Three of the parents are blah-blahing about the watermelon glut at the community garden, but Sumac's not really listening because she's busy planning the One-to-One Lottafun she and PopCorn are going to start today.

In May she and CardaMom spent a week on Haudenosaunee longhouses, and they built a mini one behind the Trampoline for Sumac's dolls to camp in. But this is going to be even more excellent because (a) it's all about the weird world of ancient Mesopotamia, and (b) PopCorn really plunges into things. Like their best One-to-One ever, when he and Sumac studied the history of weaving and how it led to the invention of computers, and they rounded up a bunch of kids to make a gigantic tapestry celebrating the Olympics all along the playground fence.

"What you making of blueberries?" Brian asks Sumac. (Her youngest sister used to be Briar, but last year, when she was three, she announced she was Brian.)

"A heptagon. That means seven sides." Sumac nudges a berry into line.

"Did we ask what a heptagon is, smarty-pants?" At ten and a half, Aspen considers it her job to crush Sumac sometimes when her sister's vocabulary gets too big for its britches.

"Mines be a face," says Brian.

"With three eyes?" Sumac examines Brian's bowl.

"Why not three eyes?"

"It's fine," says Sumac, "it's just not the normal number."

"Normal, boremal," chants Aspen, boinging higher on her ball, "peculiar's coolier."

Decisive, Brian plops another blueberry into the oatmeal. "Four eyes, because I four." Blueberries also make a straight line for a mouth; Brian doesn't smile unless it's a special occasion.

Her little sister's head is a pink-white golf ball, Sumac decides — with her neck the tee it's resting on. When the Lotterys got hair lice yet again, back in May, Brian fought off any parent who came near her with that foul shampoo, till Sumac offered to give her buzzed hair the same as PopCorn's. (Even though Sumac's only nine, she's the family barber, because she's the most accurate and undistractable.) Now Brian wants to keep her hair this short *all the days* because it means strangers don't call her a girl.

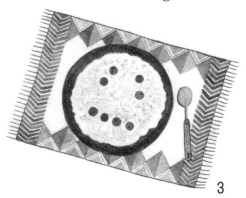

Oak, lolling in his high chair, does a grunty sort of chuckle.

Aspen grins at their baby brother and stops bouncing long enough

3

to drop another three blueberries onto the plastic plate that's Velcroed to his tray.

Sumac holds up her spoon to see if being buzzed bald would suit her too, but of course her reflection's upside down, because the spoon's con*cave*—like a cave—so it bends the light rays. She flips it around to see herself right way up on the back. Sumac happens to have more or less the same face bits as her eldest sister Catalpa, even though their ancestors come from different parts of the globe: smooth black hair and brown eyes. But it's only on Catalpa that it all adds up to beautiful, which is unfair. Sumac sticks out her tongue at her reflection and starts on her oatmeal.

PopCorn hurries into the Mess, holding his phone to his ear. "Sure, of course, the next flight." He must be talking to a stranger, because he sounds all serious and grown-up. Usually he puts on funny voices because he's the Court Jester of Camelottery.

PapaDum, ladling out seconds, raises his bushy eyebrows to ask what it's about. PapaDum's fifty-nine — that's the oldest in the whole family — so his eyebrows are getting monstrous, but he claims they're the right size to match his beard.

PopCorn nods at him, not smiling — which again makes him seem not himself. He slides the phone into the back pocket of the shorts he made from cutting the legs off

4

his favorite jeans after a chemistry experiment. "Got to go see your grandfather, poppets," he announces, sitting down between Aspen and CardaMom. Then he winces as if that hurt his butt and fishes the phone out again.

"Up to heaven?" Brian asks, big-eyed.

"No, that's *my* dad you're thinking of," MaxiMum tells her.

Aspen lets out a snigger.

Sumac glares at her sister, because it's not funny that their grandfather from Jamaica's dead, even if it did happen before most of them were alive.

Aspen can't help it, though; she was born sniggering. And MaxiMum doesn't get offended. (She says she's not naturally calm and rational, like Spock in *Star Trek*; it's from doing all that yoga.)

So PopCorn must be talking about PapaDum's father, then. "But wouldn't you just take the train if you're visiting Dada Ji in Oakville?" asks Sumac.

"I wish!" PopCorn's transferred his phone to the tiny pocket on the arm of his T-shirt, where it sticks out and waggles as he spoons up his breakfast.

"Duh," Aspen tells her, "he must be flying to Montreal to see Baba on the reserve."

"Not PapaDum's dad, nor CardaMom's," says PopCorn in an oddly flat voice. "Mine."

After a pause, CardaMom says, "You know: Iain, who PopCorn goes to see in Yukon every now and then?"

Sumac checks her mental files. "No he doesn't."

PopCorn's eyes are on his spoon as it hunts a blueberry. "Well, more like once in a blue moon."

"That grandfather's not a real one," says Aspen, lifting her feet to balance precariously on her ball. "He's just in stories about making you chop up lots of kindling when you were small."

Which sounds more like an evil sorcerer than a grandfather to Sumac.

"Oh, he's real enough," says PopCorn, licking maple syrup off one knuckle. "He just hasn't been much of a grandfather."

"To be fair," says CardaMom, "he's never even met the kids."

To be fair is one of her pet phrases, because she used to be a lawyer — the fighting-for-justice kind.

Under the table, their brown mutt, Diamond, lets out a bark for no apparent reason. She's been pining ever since the five biggest kids went to camp, and she won't cheer up till Wood's home.

Oak's trying to eat his bib. Sumac gently tugs it out of his mouth. So this fourth grandfather has been nonactivated till now, she thinks. Dormant, like a volcano. "How come you only visit your dad once in a blue moon?"

"Yukon's, ah, pretty far away," says CardaMom.

MaxiMum gives her a look. "Let's not be euphemistic."

Sumac asks, "What's —"

"Look it up," says MaxiMum, as always, because she believes people should educate themselves. "It starts *e-u*."

Sumac frowns. "Don't you like your own dad?" she asks PopCorn.

"Oh, Sumac, Queen of the Pertinent Question." He leans over to press her nose like a buzzer.

"Is *pertinent* like *impertinent*, like rude?" Aspen's eager for it not to be her getting criticized for bad manners, for once. "I *am* looking it up," she goes on, before MaxiMum can tell her to. "I'm opening up the dictionary right now. . . ." She's got MaxiMum by the ears and is pretending to read her short curls.

MaxiMum laughs, then puts on a computer-generated voice. "*Pertinent*, adjective: highly relevant to what's being talked about."

"He means Sumac's a hammer that always hits the nail on the head," says CardaMom fondly.

Sumac's not sure she likes the sound of that. Though she supposes it's better than being a hammer that hits the nail the wrong way and crumples it.

"Anyway, what did he say, hon?" PapaDum asks PopCorn.

7

"No, it was a nurse who called," PopCorn tells him. "To tell me Dad set his house on fire."

The other parents stare, and Aspen lets out an automatic burst of laughter.

"Just a small one, and he managed to put it out before the volunteer firefighters turned up."

"Poor Iain," cries CardaMom.

"Minor burns, that's about it, from the sound of it," says PopCorn.

"He play with candles?" asks Brian sternly.

PopCorn squeezes her small knee, which always has old Band-Aids dangling from it. "My dad doesn't really play. Well, anyway, so I have to get to Whitehorse today, if there's a seat, then drive to Faro. . . ."

"Hang on," says Sumac.

"Bring back presents?" asks Brian.

"Of course," PopCorn tells her, rubbing her fuzzy-peach head.

"And not New Agey ones made of braided grass, like last time," Aspen warns him.

"I'm putting you on the one-fourteen via Vancouver," murmurs CardaMom, her fingers busy on the screen of her phone. (Sumac's noticed that it's nearly always the adults who claim to have some urgent reason to break the *no electronics at meals* rule.) With her long skirts and gray-black hair down to below her butt, CardaMom can look like she's from the nineteenth century, but actually she's the techiest of the parents.

"Bless you," says PopCorn, picking up the coffeepot and filling his mug with a slosh.

"Hang on," says Sumac to him again.

But the *bless you* makes Brian do a pretend sneeze, so of course Aspen does a bigger one. Then Opal, on his perch, produces a parrot version of a sneeze, and Oak finds that so hilarious, he coughs most of a blueberry back up onto his tray.

"I think laughing may be your best talent, Oaky-doke," MaxiMum tells him with a thumbs-up.

Oak tries to do one back at her, except he forgets to let his thumb out of his fingers, so it looks like he's shaking his small fist in wrath.

MaxiMum wipes his hands, his face and double chins and neck, and the tray of his high chair. (The only thing she says she misses about working in a lab is that being a neat freak was her job, not something her loved ones mocked her for.)

"Can I get down," Aspen asks from the door, "because Slate's in my sock drawer and he misses me?"

"You haven't eaten anything, *beta*," PapaDum points out. (That's the pet name his parents called him when he was growing up in India.)

9

She pulls a face. "One more spoon?"

"Three."

Aspen runs back and shovels up her oatmeal.

"Hang on." Sumac nearly shouts it at PopCorn this time. "What about our One-to-One Lottafun?"

He blinks at her.

"You and me are doing ancient Mesopotamia, remember?"

"Sorry, sweet patoot, it'll have to be another week."

"Sumac, you could cycle to the market with me and learn, let's see, nutrition and budgeting, then in the afternoon we'll can peaches," offers PapaDum.

She scowls. One-to-Ones with PapaDum always boil down to the cooking or home repairs he was going to do anyway.

"This afternoon I'm going fern hunting with the smalls," says MaxiMum. "You could plan our hike route, put together a photo chart of the ten most common ferns in Toronto. . . ."

Sumac sees red. "You said you and me would be Mesopotamians all week," she tells PopCorn, "and put on a show with costumes and ancient snacks, and now you're going to jet off to the other side of the continent instead!"

"Sumac," says MaxiMum crisply. "It sounds like your grandfather needs a visit, and it can't wait."

She chews her lip. "Then bring me."

"Sure," says PopCorn with a shrug.

The other three adults glare.

"Whoops," he says, slapping his hand, "I mean, let me consult with my coparents."

"Not fair if Sumac flies to Yukon when she's only nine," yowls Aspen.

"Nine-going-on-nineteen, PapaDum called me the other day," Sumac tells her, "and my reading age is thirteen."

"The grandfather won't need you to read to him," says Aspen scathingly.

"Right after a fire doesn't sound like the best moment to meet PopCorn's dad," says PapaDum.

"No, it is," Sumac insists, "because two of us will be twice as cheering-up as one. I'll be totally helpful and mature."

"Come on," PopCorn tells the others, "travel's educational. Aren't we the family that likes to say why not?"

"Two seats it is, then," says CardaMom, tapping her phone.

Aspen lets out an outraged gasp.

"Don't tell me you actually want to go too," says MaxiMum.

"Well, no, but I should get something. Twenty-four hours of *Minecraft*?"

"One hour."

"Deal," says Aspen, and slips out of the Mess before anyone can object.

Diamond barks again.

"Woof," cries Oak from his high chair. He says that for Topaz and Quartz too, and even Slate: He seems to mean any four-footed animal.

But the Lotterys all clap and woof back at him because it's Oak's only word so far, and Brian's so proud of teaching it to him.

*

Grrr: PopCorn says he's too busy preparing for their trip to come to the exhibition at the Uh-Oh. But he promises Sumac she can teach him all about ancient Mesopotamia on the plane this afternoon instead.

The outing's by streetcar, subway, then foot. (The Lotterys are way too green to have a car, because it messes up the planet.) Even though it's just six of the eleven of them — because MaxiMum's at the community garden dealing with an infestation of tiny bugs called thrips — they take up the whole sidewalk. Aspen jogs backward ahead of the rest, making string figures. At Camp Jagged Falls, the kids each finger-knitted their own cat's cradle loop from Miley the Sheep's wool, but Aspen came home obsessed. It's a great fidget for her hands, though, which is useful because she's not allowed to bring Slate out in public since the Great Movie Theater Disaster. (Her rat frightens people an awful lot considering he's only twenty-seven centimeters long, not counting his tail.)

Sumac reads *How to Betray a Dragon's Hero* as she walks, because she doesn't like to waste time.

"I tired," wails Brian.

Sumac looks up and offers to play I Spy. "I spy something red . . . something stripy . . . something yucky you're about to step on!"

Brian yelps and leaps over it. "I tired again."

So then PapaDum pulls her along with the Invisible Rope, which always helps for a while. But what works best with Brian is letting her push the Oakmobile — Oak's huge stroller — which is hard to get up steps but handy to hang bags on. Pushing it must be tiring for a four-year-old, Sumac thinks. It's definitely more work for CardaMom, who has to lean over Brian and do the steering and most of the pushing while pretending she's barely touching it.

"I tired!"

"Brian, want to play Battering Ram?" says Aspen.

"Yeah!"

This involves zooming Oak at poles and garbage cans, but going around them at the last minute. Because Brian's been Oak's big sister ever since he was born, even before the two of them came to Camelottery, she sees protecting him as her job, so she'd never really ram him into anything — but sometimes she steers him away from an obstacle so sharply, his top half lolls out the other side of the Oakmobile.

Today the game lasts about a minute and a half until they nearly collide with a woman on a mobility scooter and PapaDum says "Game over" in his deep voice that there's no arguing with.

Here's the Uh-Oh, a giant crystal, all shards of glass exploding out of the street. It's really the Royal Ontario Museum, but when Brian first saw it (at two) that's what she said — "Uh-oh!" — as if somebody'd smashed a vase, so the name stuck.

Sumac stashes her book in her backpack alongside *From the Mixed-up Files of Mrs. Basil E. Frankweiler* (about kids who run away to live in a museum) and *Smile* (about dentistry, and a lot more exciting than it sounds). She always carries three, because what if you finish one and the next one sucks?

It's spookily dark inside the exhibition, with spotlights. Oak thinks it's a game and starts chortling.

"Imagine it's five thousand years ago in a desert," Sumac whispers to Brian.

"Napoleons!" Brian says it so loudly, she startles an old lady examining a carved stone. That's what Brian calls people in the past: Napoleons, because he was a famous one. She has the impression that it was Jesus and his friends the cavemen, then Napoleons, then us.

Aspen keeps on cat's cradling as she scampers between the exhibition cases. "Eiffel Tower," she announces. "Ta-dah!"

But to Sumac, her sister's string looks more like the Eiffel Tower after Godzilla's stepped on it.

She reads a list projected in light. "Wow. The Mesopotamians invented plows, cities, spoked wheels, dice, looms. . . ."

"Toy cars!" Aspen's at a touch screen. "They had tiny stone carts with a hedgehog on top, and a hole for a string so kids could pull them."

"*I* pull them," says Brian.

"It's just a picture," Aspen tells her, "but you can swipe it."

Oak wants out of his Oakmobile now. Brian gets down on the floor with him so he won't be lonely.

Oak's still not walking like all the other nearly two kids are. The parents say not to worry — that he's different, remember, but he's on track, his own track. Sumac does worry, sometimes. Luckily Oak never worries, because he has no idea he's behind. His plump bare legs keep slipping out from under him now as he wriggle-crawls across the glossy floor. CardaMom pulls his grippers (nonskid socks with the toes cut off) out of her satchel and runs to catch him, wriggling them up and over his knees.

"Look, everybody," says Aspen, "Burning House. See the flames" — her strings zigzag to and fro — "and the people flying, like the fourth grandfather."

"Fleeing, not flying." Sumac can't help it.

Aspen growls: "Sumac's spell-checking me again."

"Try and think of your sister as a help rather than a pest," CardaMom tells her.

Burning House reminds Sumac to ask, "So how did PopCorn's dad set his house on fire, anyway?"

CardaMom and PapaDum look at each other before he answers. "It was the deep fryer. Iain left sausages and fries sizzling away while he took a bath."

PopCorn can be a bit flakey, Sumac thinks; maybe he got a gene for that from his dad, just like Sic inherited PapaDum's stinky feet?

"Accidents happen," chants Aspen.

"Mostly to you," Sumac points out. The Lotterys call them *aspendents*, because they tend to leave Aspen dented. Like the Halloween before last, when she suddenly fell off her chair as if she'd been pushed by an invisible poltergeist and fractured her thumb. Only none of her family believed her for three days, because Aspen's the Girl Who Cries Wolf, always claiming to have broken things.

"Oh, oh, I have a joke about a house," says Sumac. She's been memorizing one a day. "Why did the house go to the doctor?" She waits for a count of three, like it said to in the book. "Because he had windowpanes!"

Aspen groans. "Where do jokes go to die? Sumac's mouth."

Sumac gives her the evilest scowl.

A clattering, falling sound. "Blocks!" And Aspen races off. At exhibitions, she always ends up at the build-your-own-structure-then-knock-it-down area.

Now Sumac can examine the glass cases in peace, one row at a time, reading each caption so she won't miss anything. What's inside is mostly seals — not the marine mammals, but little clay pictures you could seal up envelopes and parcels with, so you'd know if anybody'd opened them.

"Napoleons hads doggies?" That's Brian, at her side.

"Yeah," Sumac tells her, "but actually this one's a fox, and the ones underneath are sheep."

"Napoleons hads feet?" Brian examines the jagged, muddy toenails sticking out of her own sandals.

"Everyone's always had feet."

"Not fishes don't."

"Good point," says Sumac.

There's a sort of teapot that turns out to be for Mesopotamian beer, which had so much gungy stuff at the bottom that you had to drink from the top through a straw. "Possibly alcohol-free," PapaDum reads in a disappointed tone.

"They ate *date-sweetened crunchy locusts.*" Sumac recoils. "Ew!"

"Didn't you try roast locusts in Cambodia?" PapaDum asks CardaMom.

She nods. "They didn't taste that different from prawns. It would be great for the planet if we all ate bugs. . . ."

"Double ew," says Sumac.

Here's a statue of a king called Ashurnasirpal II that's no bigger than Sumac: fearsome-looking, with a beard the shape of a book and a sickle to fight demons. Then a model of something called the Great Death Pit, where sixty-eight maids were killed to honor some dead royal. Which strikes Sumac as much more ew than eating locusts. "It says the archaeologists can't agree on whether the maids volunteered to die or not," she murmurs to PapaDum.

He taps the diagram. "Notice those six guards stationed at the door. I bet the maids got *volunteered* with a knife to the throat."

So *volunteer* would be another *euphemism*. (Sumac did look it up after breakfast: It means a polite way of saying something.) There's another *e-u* word on the next panel. She reads it out: "What's a *e-u-n-u-c-h*?"

"CardaMom?" calls PapaDum. "Toss you for this one?"

Which means it must be an embarrassing question.

But CardaMom's rushing off to steer Oak away from an ancient mural of people swimming.

"Sumac!" That's Aspen shouting from somewhere up ahead.

"Somebody go shush her." CardaMom's dangling Oak upside down, his favorite position.

"Sumac!" comes the call again. "You'll love this."

A group following a tour guide with a mini Japanese flag are staring.

Sumac hurries through the rooms until she reaches Aspen. "Sh!" Sometimes her sister's like a puppy that hasn't been house-trained.

But when she reads the panel, Sumac smiles, because it says *Accountants Invented Writing*.

"Don't forget to tell Nenita and Jensen next time you see one of them," says Aspen.

There's an illustration of the way Mesopotamians wrote, little bird-foot marks in the clay. Jensen and Nenita are accountants, and Sumac's parents, biologically speaking.

They made her by mistake, and they thought they'd be terrible at being a mom and dad, and Nenita was old friends with MaxiMum, so she and Jensen agreed to give Sumac to the Lotterys the day she was born.

"What would you steal?" asks Aspen in her ear, way too loudly. "I'd go for the lion dying with all those arrows stuck in him."

Sumac winces. "OK, but you'd have to put it in your own room. I'd take . . . the giant finger with all three hundred and eighty-two of their laws written on it. It's the first time it was written down that you should assume somebody's innocent until they're proven guilty!"

Aspen's eyes roll back in her head. "Sumac Lottery, *ultimate* nerd. I'm going back to play with the little man."

"Imagic we has a lion baby," Brian's telling Oak, on the floor, pointing up at a carving of someone holding a lion cub. (The other Lotterys have sworn never to tell Brian it's actually *imagine*, because *imagic* sounds so much better.) Brian's convinced that when she and Oak are grown up they'll have babies together. Now she's taking pictures with the tablet: mostly old man statues with hair bands, buns, and braided herringbone beards. Sumac wonders if PopCorn's dad has a soft white beard like grandfathers in movies.

PapaDum's hurrying back from the exit, with Oak like an airplane pressed to his hip. "Anyone seen Aspen?"

"She was just here," says Sumac. Then, remembering: "She said something about playing with a little man."

"The museum guard?" PapaDum wonders aloud.

"Did he seem particularly short to you?" asks CardaMom, frowning.

Dread grips Sumac's stomach as she remembers: *King Ashurna-what's-his-name.*

She canters back through the exhibition, weaving in between the tourists. She finds Aspen — all alone, whew! — in the room with the three-thousand-year-old statue, making a pretty good attempt at lassoing it with her cat's cradle string. "Don't you dare!"

Aspen only giggles.

"You want us to get banned from the Uh-Oh for life?"

"Can't help it because I've got, whatchamacallit." She clicks her fingers. "Poor impulse control. So nyah!" She lassos her own foot and lifts it over her head.

"Found her" is all Sumac tells the parents when she tows Aspen back to the exit. No point giving them heart failure when it's all over.

*

"Is that all you're packing?" asks Isabella. Sprawled across the beanbag in Sumac's room, her BFF-since-diapers waves her silver-sandaled feet in the air. Isabella always looks as if she's ready for a party, maybe because she's an only child; her mami doesn't let her leave the apartment in just shorts no matter how hot it gets. She wouldn't have lasted two days at Camp Jagged Falls, where Sumac and her English cousin-she'd-never-met-before Seren Johnson ran around literally caked with mud and loved it.

"We're only going to be in Yukon for two nights," Sumac tells Isabella.

"Won't you freeze?" asks Isabella.

Sumac laughs. "It's July there too, nutcase." She rolls a pair of leggings into a neat sausage. "I bet we'll see moose and bear and elk, and these special sheep they've got with curly horns."

"What if PopCorn takes you somewhere glamorous?" asks Isabella. He's been Isabella's favorite of the Lottery parents ever since he threw her a surprise *Fancy Nancy* tea party for her third birthday.

"This is like a mission of mercy," Sumac reminds her. "We only have one day to find his burned dad somewhere new to live and cheer him up. I'm the first of the grandkids

22

he'll ever have met." It strikes her that this means she'll probably always be his pet.

"You're such a tidy packer," sighs Isabella, dangling her head over Sumac's sock drawer. "Can I move in and be you while you're gone?"

Sumac does love her room: the translucent canopy over her bed that makes her feel royal, the high shelf for all the dolls she's been collecting since Baba — CardaMom's dad — made her a baby one in a birch bark canoe, the rainbow duvet cover, the alphabetized bookcase where every week she turns one of her favorite jackets face out. (Right now it's *Wonder*.) She contemplates the painted sky that goes right across the walls and ceiling, with fluffy clouds that took PopCorn weeks to get right, and the sun coming up on the door. There's only one window, but it looks out at the catalpa tree that presses huge, heart-shaped leaves against the glass.

"Hey, Topaz," calls Isabella. The cat pushes through the slightly open door and jumps onto her lap, purring so loudly she vibrates. She's exactly the same orange as PopCorn's topaz pinky ring that he found in a plug hole in Argentina. "Where's your sister?"

"Quartz must be around somewhere," says Sumac.

"Go on, admit it, is Quartz your imaginary sister?" Isabella asks the cat.

"She's just shy." Maybe because of the rock they named her after, Sumac thinks: Quartz can be so colorless and clear, it's almost invisible.

They hear the clang of the cowbell. Isabella leaps up as if she's been electrocuted, and the cat springs to the floor.

"Aren't you staying for lunch?" Sumac asks, deadpan. "I thought you wanted to be me for two days."

"Yeah, but what if PapaDum's made his kale salad?"

"It didn't kill you last time."

"Nearly," says Isabella as she hurries into the Hall of Mirrors, checking her braid-of-braids in the most elaborate gilt one. "Kale's a bush, not a food."

It's all a matter of what you're used to, Sumac supposes. Like, Isabella's Colombian, so she loves that disgusting cake they soak in evaporated milk, condensed milk, and cream. "Come for a double sleepover on the weekend," she tells Isabella, "and I promise there'll be hot dogs."

"Hey, a new quote," says her friend, pointing to PopCorn's loopy letters in wet-erase marker across a tall mirror: Some days you're the pigeon, some days you're the statue. "What's that about?" And then, as Sumac grins, Isabella says, "Oh, OK, OK, I get it."

CHAPTER 2

- - - - - - - - - - - - - - - - - - - -

THE TRIP

"They used stone carpets that never wore out," Sumac tells PopCorn.

"Practical, if not cozy." He's reclined his seat already, though it's lunchtime and the plane hasn't even taken off. "Ancient Mesopotamia is Iraq now, yeah?"

"Some of Iraq," she says, correcting him, "and some of Iran and Kuwait as well. Their language is called Sumerian because the southern half was called the land of Sumer."

"Sounds like it should be your homeland."

Sumac nods, grinning. "Especially since they called themselves *saggiga*, the black-headed people," she says, pointing to her hair. "Oh, something I like is, Mesopotamians counted in sixties, not in tens. Look —" She lifts PopCorn's nearer hand. "Use your thumb to count the . . . the . . . there's a special word for the finger sections —"

"Phalanges," he supplies.

It sounds like *falafel*. "The *phalanges* on that hand," she says with difficulty, "go on, count them."

PopCorn does. "Twelve." Pleased with himself, because he's terrible at math.

"Then on the other hand, you curl a finger over for each twelve, which makes sixty," Sumac explains, "and that's why we count seconds and minutes in sixties; we're copying the Mesopotamians."

"Too complicated," he groans, putting on his eye mask and lying back like a movie star.

The plane's full of adults traveling on their own and regular small-sized families. If all the Lotterys were here, it strikes Sumac, they'd take up a row and a half. "So what's wrong with your dad?"

"Don't really know yet," says PopCorn. "Apart from the burns, possibly smoke inhalation. . . ."

"No, I mean, why don't you like him enough to visit except once in a blue moon?"

Her father lets out a long breath. "It's more the other way around, peanut."

The dad doesn't like his own son? But everybody likes PopCorn, even the Lotterys' scowly letter carrier.

27

"Sometimes two people can be related without really . . . clicking," he murmurs. "Dad's pretty conservative."

That puzzles Sumac. "You mean like for voting in elections?"

"Set in his ways. He prefers things how they were, or at least how they seemed to be when he was eight instead of eighty-two."

Sumac subtracts seventy-four from this year. World War II and no Internet: Who could prefer that?

"Hi, sweetie," says a flight attendant with too much blusher on. "Where's your mom today?"

"I've got two," Sumac tells her. "One of them is practicing aikido, and the other is running a free legal advice clinic. Also another dad who's minding my siblings and making something called mulligatawny soup."

"Lucky you," the woman answers in a slightly nervous voice. "Would you like a Junior Activity Pack?"

Sumac glances at the flat square wrapped in plastic with the usual five scratchy crayons. "No thanks. We're going to be studying Sumerian; it's the oldest written language in the world."

"Lovely," says the flight attendant, and hurries on down the plane.

Sumac wonders if that sounded a bit show-offy. She was just answering a question, not boasting. She doesn't actually have anything to boast about, because she hasn't learned more than a couple of Sumerian words yet.

Her and PopCorn's challenge for this afternoon is to learn ten phrases from the minibook Sumac spent her allowance on at the museum, but he keeps thinking *ses* means sister when actually it's brother. The one phrase he manages to remember is a proverb, *Nuzu egalla bacar*, because it means *Ignoramuses are numerous in the palace*, and that cracks him up. "Fewer brain cells," he says, tapping his head, "so I need laughter as the glue to make the information stick."

But today PopCorn's not laughing half as much as he usually does, Sumac notices. Not even when he puts in earbuds and watches a comedy with a lot of crashing and falling.

✳

It's exciting to be the only kid coming along on PopCorn's homecoming trip . . . but it's not actually a very exciting trip so far. Nine hours in the air, five hours in the rental car, and all the time the Yukon sky stays white because they're so far north. Sumac conks out in the backseat before she's seen anything interesting at all, and barely wakes when PopCorn carries her into the B&B.

In the morning the sun's high already, and PopCorn's walking around talking on the phone to somebody called

Melissa. "The thing is, Melissa, I fly back to Toronto tomorrow and my dad needs to see the doctor on an urgent basis, so how do you suggest we might solve this?"

Sumac stops listening and pulls *The Popularity Papers: Book Seven* out of her backpack.

At breakfast it turns out she and PopCorn are the only two people staying in the B&B. The clock on the wall has numbers that face backward and the hands aren't moving; it says *Relax, You're on Yukon Time.* It's fun choosing from all the different little boxes of cereal — Sumac mixes brightly colored loops with chocolatey ones shaped like rockets — but they taste kind of sickening. PopCorn doesn't have any, just so much coffee that his hands shake.

The view out the window's like a painting: mountains and grass, no people. "Where's Faro?"

"This is it," PopCorn tells her with an odd kind of smile. "Population four hundred on a busy day. When I was your age, it had the biggest open-pit lead and zinc mine in the world, but then the mine shut down."

"Wow. Four hundred, that's . . . almost nobody."

On the way to the grandfather's, Sumac watches for wildlife but only spots a crow.

"More moose than humans live around here. I spotted two near the highway last night," says PopCorn.

"You should have woken me!"

He shakes his head. "As you'll learn if you have your own, my love, rule number one of parenthood is *never wake a sleeping child.*"

There's an old man on a porch who seems to be making a chair out of skinny branches. Sumac hasn't seen any children in Faro yet. PopCorn drives across water with canoeists shooting down it, which reminds her: "Hey, we saw this mural of Mesopotamians escaping across a river holding inflated animal skins, like personal flotation devices."

"Crafty," murmurs PopCorn, in an absentminded way. He turns sharply into a driveway and shuts the motor off. *"Vel,"* he says in his best Transylvanian accent, *"velcome* to my humble childhood home."

Sumac thought it would be a log cabin, maybe, or quaint, at least. But it's just a regular kind of ugly house.

PopCorn presses the end of her nose. "Beep!"

She slaps him away. "Why do you *do* that?"

"Because it's cute as a button." He does it again before she can ward him off. Then he drumrolls on his shorts and calls out like in Hide and Seek: "Ready or not, here we come. . . ."

The front door's not locked.

As soon as they step into the hall, the stink of smoke gets into Sumac's throat.

"Dad?" calls PopCorn.

No answer.

"You wait outside so you're not breathing in the toxins," he tells Sumac.

She's glad to retreat to the front yard and read in the sunshine.

PopCorn comes out about ten minutes later talking about drywall with Frankenstein's monster. Well, a tall, bony old man in steel-capped work boots, jeans, and a flannel shirt that looks unbearably hot, balding, with gray hair, no eyebrows (just little scratchy bits) and a straggly gray beard. His nose is all swollen with red-and-purple lines across it, and his hands are bandaged.

You shouldn't judge on appearances, Sumac reminds herself.

The grandfather stares at her.

PopCorn breaks off to say, in an oddly formal way, "Dad, this is Sumac."

"Smack?"

"*Su*mac." He leans on the first syllable. "Like the tree. The fourth of our seven."

"Fifth," says Sumac, correcting him, but the word hardly comes out, she's so nervous suddenly. "Hi."

The old man's eyes are shifting between the two of them and Sumac can read his mind: She and PopCorn don't actually look related, because her ancestors are from the Philippines and Germany, and his are Scottish all the way back.

"OK. Well, they're expecting you, expecting us, at the nursing center, Dad," says PopCorn, "so we'd better head over."

"I was seen to the night before last." The grandfather holds up one bandaged hand like an Egyptian mummy. His voice is hoarse, with an accent as strong as if he never left Glasgow.

"The dressing probably needs changing, and I've managed to wangle you an appointment with the doctor."

"I'm all right." He makes a checking-his-watch movement, but the bandage is in the way. "I play golf, the mornings."

"Not this morning," murmurs PopCorn, opening the passenger door for him.

"I'll take my own car, thank you."

"C'mon, Dad, why waste the gas?"

The rumbling volcano hasn't said one word to Sumac yet. Has he already decided not to like her, because he doesn't like PopCorn and she's his daughter? Or maybe — it occurs to her — because she's adopted, so she doesn't have any of the grandfather's genes? Disliking in advance, that's prejudice. She climbs into the back.

At the nursing center, the three of them wait, wait, wait in a waiting room where the books are ridiculously kiddish and the coloring book of *Creatures of Yukon* is all scribbled over already.

The grandfather stares into space. He fiddles with the packet of cigarettes the nurse has reminded him twice that he's not allowed to light up here. He's got a horrible phlegmy cough; Sumac wonders whether it's from smoking or whether he breathed in poisonous fumes from the fire.

PopCorn buys chocolate from a vending machine; it tastes as if it's been melting and hardening over and over since Mesopotamian times.

The grandfather bursts out: "Load of nonsense."

"The doctor's only here twice a month," says PopCorn again, "so I guess he has to see the urgent cases first."

"I play golf, the mornings."

Sumac's quizzed herself on all the difficult spellings from the coloring book: cougar, musk ox, white-footed deer mouse, pine marten, ptarmigan with its silent *p*. She considers spelling her name Psumac from now on. *Psumac, Queen of the Land of Ancient Psumer.* That's nearly as pretty a name as Seren, which is the prettiest Sumac knows; it means *star* in Welsh. Her cousin Seren Johnson has the hugest laugh, and loves singing and acting, and Sumac hopes she'll remember to message Sumac from England like she promised.

At the bottom of the book box she finds a crumpled leaflet called *Fun for All in Faro*. "There's an arboretum that *showcases the wonders of native flora and fauna.*"

PopCorn doesn't look up from the screen of his phone. "Let's see how much time we've got at the end of the day."

"And a sheep center where you can see those special sheep with the curly horns. . . ."

"Don't nag, Sumac."

She wasn't! She was only mentioning some things they could do when all this boring stuff is over.

"Those fellows are all up the mountain, this time of year."

She turns to the grandfather. "Who are?"

"The sheep."

Sumac tries to keep the conversation going. "What I'm really longing to see is the northern lights. I watched this show about them once, how the oxygen ions make the green and the nitrogen ones make the orange. Did you know the Inuit believed the lights could kidnap children?"

"Not in summer."

Sumac blinks at him.

"You won't see the lights. Sky's too bright."

Oh. So much for that, then.

PopCorn carries on swiping his screen and biting the skin around his thumbnail.

All the grandfather has said to Sumac so far is two things she can't do. She supposes he's trying to make sure she won't be disappointed when she doesn't see the special sheep and the northern lights, but still, he's not exactly a sparkling conversationalist. Maybe PopCorn got that talent from his mother, who died years ago, or maybe it's all his own.

She tries again, pulling the tablet out of her backpack. "Want to see some pictures of the rest of your grandchildren?"

The old man doesn't say no, at least.

The ones from the exhibition yesterday are all blurry, of course; that's what happens when you let the four-year-old take the photos. (It's one of Sumac's jobs to edit and file all the family pictures.) She clicks on *Erase all taken on same date*, then flicks back through July and June to find some good ones. "That's Sic, my biggest brother, he's sixteen," she says, with a pang of missing him.

The grandfather squints at the screen. "The one with the clown hair?"

"It's called an Afro." Though knowing Sic, he'd probably like the sound of *clown hair*.

"Why would a person want to be called that?"

"Sic? Oh, it's not *sick*, like vomit — it's *S-i-c*," Sumac explains. "That's a special word you put in square brackets after something that looks nuts, to tell readers you really did mean it that way."

His watery eyes blink once, twice.

Sumac finds a group shot taken in the back of the Wild behind Camelottery. "There's Catalpa, she's the next oldest." In black, with a coffin-shaped zipper bag over her shoulder, rolling her eyes; it's as if Catalpa woke up on her fourteenth birthday and decided everything was exhausting. (Whereas nine, like Sumac, is just the right age, because you're not confused by everything the way a little kid like Brian is, but your brain hasn't been rotted away by hormones yet.) "The one poking Catalpa with a branch is Wood, that's short for Redwood, because when he was born the parents thought his hair was going to be red, but it turned out brown. Here's Aspen, with Brian on her back — used to be Briar — and that's Oak, he's our baby." Oak looks so adorable with his foot in Wood's mouth, playing Alligator Attack.

"Very hippy-dippy," says the old man with something that could be a snort or a sniff.

"What is?"

"Trees."

"I guess names have to come from somewhere. What did — what were you named after?" asks Sumac. "I mean for."

"A saint, was it, Dad?" That's PopCorn.

His father furrows his brow.

"Saint Iain? Or hang on, didn't you have an uncle Iain?"

The old man doesn't answer.

Desperate for something to talk about, Sumac flicks through the pictures till she finds a close-up of Camelottery. "And this is where we live. It was built in the days of Queen Victoria, but the frilly redbrick style is called Queen Anne."

She's always found that funny, but the grandfather doesn't seem to.

"When I was small Wood totally lied to me that it's called Camelottery because camels used to live there before us. I mean, we really do call it Camelottery, but because of Camelot. King Arthur's castle?"

His long face doesn't show whether he's ever heard of King Arthur.

"The turrets and gargoyles, did you notice them?" Sumac zooms in on her favorite gargoyle, the one that's sticking out its tongue. "And also, of course, Camel*lottery* because of our, all of our surname." She's pretty sure that's bad grammar.

The grandfather reacts at last, turning to PopCorn. "You're a Miller, same as me."

"I changed it, Dad, remember?"

The old man takes out his cigarettes again, but the receptionist points to the sign on the wall, so he puts them back.

"He's not a very good listener." Sumac whispers it right into PopCorn's ear, so as not to hurt the grandfather's feelings.

Instead of answering, PopCorn shows her a website he's looking at on his phone. *Symptoms of Smoke Inhalation*, it says at the top. She follows his fingertip. *Cough, shortness of breath, hoarseness, headache, confusion.* He taps the last word.

Ah, so that's it: The grandfather's confused because of smoke in his head.

Sumac turns back to the old man with her most helpful face on. "All four of the parents changed their surnames when we won the lottery, see?"

Definitely a snort this time. "Advertising their business to the world!"

Sumac is puzzled, because it wasn't a business. "No, they just wanted a new name to share with Sic. MaxiMum was walking up and down the corridor in the hospital, with CardaMom and PopCorn and PapaDum all rubbing her back, which was hurting because Sic was taking his sweet time to come out of her" — Sumac's always liked that phrase, *taking his sweet time*, she can just imagine her big brother in miniature form, lounging around on the placenta — "and CardaMom picked up a lottery ticket off the floor to use as a bookmark. She was reading a book

40

called *A Supposedly Fun Thing I'll Never Do Again*," Sumac adds, because the title always sticks in her mind. "Anyway, the ticket had the winning number on it, and after three months, when the company still couldn't find the real winner, they had to give the money to us. So the parents decided we'd be the Lotterys, because they felt so lucky now they had Sic. Especially since the money meant they could buy a big house to fill with lots more kids, and do interesting stuff with us all day instead of going to work."

PopCorn is grinning at her. "Sumac's the keeper of the family stories, even the ones that happened before she was born."

The old man breaks his silence. "Our ancestor must have had a mill."

Sumac's bewildered for a second. Oh, right: Miller.

"Or at least lived near one," says PopCorn.

"Nae," snaps his father, "he'd have owned it."

They lapse into silence again until the nurse finally calls, "Iain Miller."

✱

Their one day in Yukon has been a total washout. So far Sumac and PopCorn don't seem to have cheered up the grandfather at all, or found him a new place to live. All they've done is go to the doctor and the drugstore.

The grandfather doesn't want to come for ice cream with them. He says he has things to do, thank you very much.

It's vanilla or chocolate; there aren't any of Sumac's favorites, like blood orange or toasted pine nut or chai spice. PopCorn barely eats half of his. He says jet lag is hard on the stomach.

"So how do they suck the smoke back out of your dad?" Sumac wants to know.

PopCorn shakes his head. "It turns out he doesn't have smoke inhalation, just a regular old smoker's cough."

"Oh. Do you want to hear more about the Mesopotamians?"

"Later, I'd love to," he tells her, dumping the rest of his cone in the garbage, "but right now I have to call someone called a regional care program supervisor."

Sumac folds her arms.

As they're driving back to the B&B, PopCorn says, "Sorry the ice cream wasn't much good."

"I don't care about the ice cream!" Does he think she's a baby?

"OK, petal."

"So much for our special, exciting, One-to-One Lottafun," she says in a wobbly voice. "This is turning out to be a big old Zerofun."

PopCorn pulls over so fast the wheels screech. Sumac braces herself in case they're going to crash.

He parks almost in the ditch. "Look, a gold pan!"

"What? Where?"

It's a broken, blue plastic Frisbee.

"Use your imagination," says PopCorn. "I'm going to teach you to pan for gold like a hundred years ago."

This turns out to mean standing in an icy creek collecting a lot of black sand with not a single speck of gold.

After about a quarter of an hour, Sumac's feet are killing her. "No offense, but I'm not enjoying this."

"Me neither," admits PopCorn. "And it strikes me now that the water's probably laced with contaminants from the mine. Sorry it didn't *pan* out."

Sumac moans, because PopCorn's puns are the worst.

He clambers out and starts rubbing his feet on the grass to dry them. "Faro makes me feel fourteen again."

Sumac thought adults were always wanting to be young again, but PopCorn says it kind of grimly.

Back in their B&B, when he finishes leaving one message (for someone called a chief geriatrician) and starts dialing again, Sumac asks quickly, "Why does being conservative mean your dad doesn't like us?"

PopCorn presses the red button to cancel the call. "He doesn't not like you, munchkin. He doesn't know you yet."

Sumac's chewing her lip as if it's licorice.

"Basically, the old buffer's ticked off that I married a man instead of a woman."

She stares. "But that was donkey's years ago." What, more than twenty? In the last century, anyway. Which is a long time to stay mad.

"Yeah, well, it's hard to teach a dumb old donkey new tricks," says PopCorn, and adds a pretty convincing hee-haw.

Not as good as Aspen would do it, but it makes Sumac grin.

Then PopCorn says he needs to go in the bathroom and have a Dull Conversation with the other parents by Skype before they're all in bed, even though it's only seven here in Yukon and the sun's still high in the sky.

A Dull Conversation means an Adult Conversation, because Sic once heard the phrase wrong. Sic got to make up most of the family slang just by being born first, which isn't fair, but there you go.

Sumac's listening to her summertime playlist, but she presses pause when PopCorn's voice goes up. "I *know* it's a lot for you all to take in," he's saying, "and I've no right to spring it on you like this, it's just that I'm in such a state, I can't — a score of twenty-two counts as mild, but still, if that's what it is, it's only going to get worse."

Sumac wonders what's *a lot to take in*, and what PopCorn scored twenty-two at. Technically she's eavesdropping, but it's because she's stressed and she needs more information so she can calm down.

"Only for a while, obviously, just to get him properly checked out and see what the options are. . . . You've frozen, hon." That must be PapaDum he's talking to. PopCorn lets out a growl of frustration.

Nothing for a minute. Then CardaMom's voice, shouting: "— hear us?"

"Just audio, no video. This Wi-Fi's pathetic," PopCorn tells her.

"I was asking, what about a live-in?" That's PapaDum, gruff.

"No, I suggested two of them, working in shifts, and Dad completely freaked out about strangers under his roof."

A silence. "We'd be strangers too." MaxiMum's calm voice.

"We're his *family*," protests CardaMom.

Sumac wonders how the Lotterys can count as this grandfather's family when they live five thousand kilometers away and he's never met most of them.

"Only in a technical sense," says MaxiMum.

"Do you have to sound like such a robot?" CardaMom roars at her.

At this point, Sumac puts her music on again, fast, because when sibs argue it doesn't really matter, it's just like weather, but when parents do it —

She listens grimly to two and a half tracks about walking on sunshine and fish jumping and cotton growing high.

Finally PopCorn comes out of the bathroom wearing a crooked kind of smile and says, "Guess what? We're going to bring my dad home with us for a visit."

Sumac tries to look pleasantly surprised.

CHAPTER 3

- - - - - - - - - - - - - - - - - - - -

DAY ONE

At seven the next evening, PopCorn pushes open the front door of Camelottery. "Greetings, earthlings!" Sumac's behind the grandfather, looking at the worn-down heels of his boots.

Limbs flailing, knocking a long mirror askew, Aspen gets to PopCorn first and jumps to hang around his neck.

"You brung presents?" asks Brian, behind her.

PopCorn says, "Ah . . ."

Sumac's face falls. They completely forgot.

"Where the presents?" demands Brian.

"I've got half a candy necklace," Sumac offers.

"We've brought my dad," says PopCorn, too brightly,

47

gesturing toward the old man in a ta-dah way. "Everybody, this is Iain. Your fourth grandfather."

Brian stares balefully. "That not a present. Where his eyebrows?"

Sumac tries to distract her with the candy necklace.

Brian scowls but puts it around her neck. "Where is they?" she asks again.

"They got burned off in the fire," Sumac whispers in her ear, because it's a family rule that there are no stupid questions.

PopCorn sniffs at Aspen. "Is that nail polish remover I smell?"

She nods. "We superglued our index fingers to our thumbs as an experiment."

"An experiment in what, frustration?"

"To figure out how much humans rely on opposable thumbs," said MaxiMum, coming into the hall. "Hello, Iain."

"Welcome, welcome," cries CardaMom, hurrying downstairs wearing Oak on her shoulders. "PapaDum," she calls toward the Mess, "stop chopping onions, they're here."

The grandfather looks from one face to the next, and suddenly Sumac is glad the three eldest kids are still away at camp, because compared with Faro, Yukon, the Lotterys are looking like a crowd already.

"Could you do with a rest, Iain?" asks CardaMom, bouncing on the spot to keep Oak happy.

The visitor doesn't say anything, just clears his throat in a wet, rattly way.

"A drink?"

"Hi, Iain." Here comes PapaDum, drying his hands on a cloth. There's a pause, and then he asks, "Who's hungry?"

"Slate is," says Aspen, pulling her rat out of her hoodie pocket.

The old man squints. "Is that what it looks like?"

"Meet Slate Frisby. Technically he's an odd-eyed hooded American blue dumbo satin." Aspen balances him on her palm and kisses his nose. "Frisby for *Mrs. Frisby and the Rats of NIMH*, and Slate because he's gray except for his white tummy, see?"

The grandfather recoils from the tiny paws.

"Put him away," says MaxiMum.

Aspen stuffs Slate in her pocket. "Och, noo, I nearly forgot, I've got tricks to show ye," she says in what Sumac realizes is a really bad imitation of the grandfather's Scottish accent. Aspen clutches one hand in the other and clambers through the loop, but too fast, so she topples over and smacks her face on the banisters.

Typical, thinks Sumac, gritting her teeth.

A few minutes later, when Aspen's got a bag of frozen peas pressed to her cheek, they all go into the Mess.

Brian's helping PapaDum make guacamole and spattering it all over herself as she brings the masher down: "Mush, mash, smush . . ."

"Dinner in ten," says PapaDum.

"I'm leading the tour," Aspen insists, in her own accent again. She scurries ahead. "Look, this is our Gym-Jo, it's a gym and a dojo for aikido all in one," she tells the grandfather. "Sumac sleeps in here" — flinging the door open and not bothering to shut it — "and this is the Mud Room" — a havoc of rubber boots, scooters, Rollerblades, Hula-Hoops, and skipping ropes — "and the Can-Do for if you need to pee, do you need to pee by any chance?"

MaxiMum looks at her without saying anything, which shuts Aspen up.

"These baby gates are tricky," says CardaMom, edging ahead of the visitor, "you have to press this bit down while you pull the whole thing up. Oh, and mind the treadmill desk," she says as they reach the second floor, dipping her knees so Oak's face doesn't hit the feather mobile. "It takes up half the landing, but it's *so* good for hearts and lungs."

Sumac studies the grandfather's long denim legs from behind. Surely if he tried running on their treadmill, they'd snap like dead branches?

"Another bathroom here, Iain," says MaxiMum, tapping the door marked *The Roman Bath* in carved-looking lettering. They can hear PopCorn having a cold shower, but not singing Broadway songs the way he usually does. "This next one's our Theater, and this turquoise room is Brian and Oak's — our little ones."

Aspen's shaking her bag of peas like a maraca now.

"Then we sleep just in here" — CardaMom does that wave of a finger between her and MaxiMum that means the moms are the *we* — "and PopCorn and PapaDum in that room over there."

"Who?" The word comes out of the old man suddenly, like the hoot of an owl.

"PopCorn, your son, remember?" says Sumac very clearly. She wonders if the grandfather's confused again. Maybe there was some smoke in his head that the doctor couldn't see?

"My son's Reginald," the grandfather corrects her.

"Sorry, silly parent nicknames," CardaMom says in a rush, "but they've stuck."

Reginald sounds a lot sillier than PopCorn, in Sumac's opinion.

"Mm, we'd had way too much tequila the night we picked them," says MaxiMum.

The old man's lizard eyes flick over the Lotterys as he pulls his cigarettes out of his shirt pocket.

"Ah, yeah," says CardaMom. Which is her way of saying no. She fiddles with her long gray-black braid, retying the end.

"No smoky," chants Brian.

"Not in the house, but in the yard is fine," says MaxiMum. "I have one a day myself."

Sumac will never understand why someone as good at self-control as MaxiMum can't give up that horrible habit completely.

The old man puts his cigarettes back in his pocket. Then, in CardaMom's direction: "Any chance of a cup of tea?"

"Sure, Iain. And dinner won't be long. Will we just show you the rest of the house first?"

"Had my dinner on the plane."

"I'll put the kettle on for tea," says MaxiMum, heading downstairs.

"Let's just stash your bags, then." CardaMom leads the way up to the third floor, past the big kids' rooms.

Aspen goes into the Loud Lounge muttering something about finding her Slinky and forgets to come back.

Up to the attic. "We've got you in Spare Oom just for tonight," says CardaMom, "but we'll work out something better for you in the morning."

Spare Oom is a bit spidery, but — Sumac thinks — not half as bad as the creepy Overspill down in the basement, which the Lotterys only use when they've accidentally said yes to too many visitors.

They leave the grandfather there to settle in.

"Doesn't have much to say, does he?" Aspen joins them on the stairs, wearing her Slinky around her neck like an Elizabethan ruff.

"He's probably exhausted, and a bit shy," says CardaMom under her breath.

*

The visitor doesn't come down to breakfast the next morning. PapaDum brings a tray up to the attic.

They're having eggs fried in holes in bread. Sumac moves the little toast lid over her moon so it goes from full, to crescent, to dark. The Lotterys are arguing about whether propping your knees on the table (Aspen) is as bad as taking chewed food out of your mouth to look at (Brian).

The four parents need to have another Dull Conversation after breakfast, apparently. MaxiMum challenges the kids to spend the time coming up with a list of table manners, "so we don't appall your grandfather too much."

"On the Trampoline," suggests Aspen.

"I'll get nauseous if I have to bounce and write at the same time," says Sumac.

So she takes down the manners neatly in the Tree Fort, with Brian practicing Downward Dog, while Aspen repeatedly climbs up the ladder and out the window, dangles from the rope, and drops onto the grass. Sumac writes:

No books/screens/earbuds at meals

No insulting the cooking

No whining or squabbling

No eating like dogs

No hoarding, gobbling, overstuffing, or making yourself puke from overeating

No dangling food (higher than chin level)

No flicking/throwing/stealing

No facing backward, lying down, or eating
upside down

No wiping hands on clothes (yours/
anyone else's)

No burping/farting on purpose

When the three kids have gotten bored and started talking about tapeworms instead, CardaMom knocks on the ladder. She passes Oak to them like a parcel through the window so she can take their list and see what they've come up with. "Feeding time at the zoo," she murmurs.

"Is it not a good list?" asks Sumac, a bit offended.

"It's great, in a stomach-turning way," says CardaMom. "You've included every possible disgusting behavior."

"Not *every*," calls Aspen from the swinging rope. "I can think of way disgustinger things to do at meals, like —"

"Spare us," interrupts CardaMom.

On the rug that covers the Tree Fort's splintery floor, Oak lays his face on his foot, watching dust motes in a beam of sunlight.

"It's just that it's all put rather negatively. What about some recommendations?"

"Like, instead of *no eating like dogs*," says Aspen, "what about *eat like human beings?*"

"Which ones, though?" Sumac wants to know.

"Great point." CardaMom nods. "Polite in France is rude in Japan."

"What I meant was, obviously, *don't stick your face right into your bowl, Aspen*," says Sumac.

"Nobody minds when Diamond does it" comes Aspen's voice from outside, panting a little.

"Different rules for different species: agreed?" says CardaMom. "What else could we put more positively?"

"*Burp and fart . . . accidentally*," suggests Aspen, and Brian joins in the sniggering.

"Let's just leave that one out," murmurs CardaMom.

Sumac goes into Camelottery to cool down a bit. She needs PopCorn so they can finally start properly on being Mesopotamians. (She tried to give him a quiz on nouns on the airplane while the grandfather was snoring, but he only scored three out of twenty.) On the Where Board by the front door, opposite PopCorn's name she reads Ðiniэ w. Clээ, and she gets quite excited because that must be a secret message for her in Sumerian . . . but finally she figures out it's just "Clinic with Dad" in his atrocious handwriting.

Up in the Bookery at the top of the house, Sumac looks up pictures of Mesopotamian sculptures. A friend of a cousin of PapaDum's from Ukraine who stayed a week with the Lotterys painted the ceiling to say thank you. (Her friend Isabella's so scared of the mural, she won't go into the Bookery.) It makes you think you're right inside a book, like an illustration coming to life, with the pages being fanned open by a pair of giant hands.

The door of Spare Oom is shut, so Sumac can't see if it looks any different now the grandfather's sleeping there.

One floor down, in the Loud Lounge, PapaDum and MaxiMum are frowning at a laptop while Aspen and CardaMom teach Brian to Hula-Hoop. Brian tries spinning her hoop around her tiny waist, but it only goes around one and a half times before it drops.

"We've been learning mensa," Aspen tells Sumac over her shoulder.

PapaDum lets out a snort.

"*Dementia*, which is the brain problem your grandfather may have," CardaMom corrects her. "*Mensa's* the opposite: a club for people with too many brains, like a few poseurs I knew in law school."

"*The 3 Rs: Stay Relaxed, Reassuring, Respectful*," PapaDum reads off the screen.

Sumac goes over to see. At the top it says *Learning Unit 1.1. Alzheimer's and Other Dementias: Caring for Your Loved One.*

But this old man isn't their *loved one.* Sumac doesn't suppose he's anyone's loved one, not anymore, since PopCorn's mom has been dead for more than thirty years. Unless he has some best friends back in Faro?

Brian tries to spin the hoop again, moving in a huge circle, but she's too slow, so it drops.

"Can you recap the video for Sumac?" MaxiMum asks Aspen.

Who always goes slightly cross-eyed when she's trying to remember things. "These kids were crying, boohoo, because their mensa — their *dementia*ed granny couldn't remember their names anymore blah blah blah, but then they did a scrapbook with her, The End."

"That's a bit harsh," protests CardaMom.

"Hey, at least I was listening!"

"Dementia sounds like the dementors in *Harry Potter,*" says Sumac. Poor guy and all that, but this fourth grandfather has only just learned their names; they barely know him, so she doesn't see that they have much reason to be boohooing.

CardaMom offers Oak a Hula-Hoop on his left side. (Oak's physiotherapist is always nagging them to work his left arm and leg so they'll get as strong as his right ones.) "Well, one thing we could take from the video is that Iain will probably be more interested in talking about the past than the present."

But that's true of all oldies, thinks Sumac. Or even middlies: the parents are always going on about the wild times they had back in the day, meaning the end of the last century.

"I'm practicing all my best tricks for him, because they had acrobats back in ye olden times," says Aspen, knotting her hands behind her and climbing through them.

"You going to show your grandfather your tricks, Oakydoke?" PapaDum asks.

"Watch *my* trick." Brian grimaces with effort, but her hoop plummets almost at once. She kicks it across the room, her mouth trembling.

"Want to try Teacup again?" says Aspen, throwing her a cat's cradle string.

"Look, I do Teacup," Brian tells Sumac, her fingers knotted together with the wool.

"And Owl Eyes, nearly," says Aspen, "except they're a bit squinty."

PapaDum reads aloud, *"The home should ideally be small, modern, and all on one level. The environment should be structured and predictable."*

CardaMom snorts. "That's like all that stuff about babyproofing in the parenting books, and we chucked those out the window the day Sic was born."

"Which window?" Aspen asks, excited. "A high one? The Artic?" Slate's pointy face appears in the neck of her pajamas.

"Chucked, metaphorically," says MaxiMum. She taps the screen. "*He slash she will require a lifestyle of routine and calm.* Does that sound like Camelottery?"

Fair point, thinks Sumac. The only routine here is, wake up and decide what you want to learn.

"This is the bit that worries me," mutters PapaDum.

"Mm," says MaxiMum, nodding.

Sumac goes over to see what they're reading. *If you have always had a difficult or lacking relationship with the impaired relative*, it says, *such a move could be inadvisable in the extreme.*

"Does that mean if the grandfather's drunk?"

"What?"

"Ah yes, impaired, like impaired driving," says MaxiMum with a grin. "No, it means that the dementia, if that's what it is, is muddling his thinking — like drink can, I suppose."

"Basically, it seems he's starting to lose his marbles," says PapaDum.

Aspen does one of her inappropriate mad laughs.

"I hadded marbles," says Brian sorrowfully.

"PapaDum doesn't mean those little glass balls," says Sumac. He should remember that Brian's too young for metaphors.

"We putted them away for Oak not eating," says Brian.

"The grandfather's brains are *like* that, like your marbles," CardaMom tells her, "not actual marbles."

"What does *inadvisable* mean?" Sumac asks.

"This website would advise against PopCorn bringing his dad here," says MaxiMum, "because they've never got on very well."

CardaMom blows a raspberry. "This website lacks imagination. I think it's going to be just what Iain and PopCorn need: very healing."

PapaDum rolls his eyes.

"Besides, what else are we supposed to do? It's an emergency."

"Wah wah wah wah," Brian wails like an ambulance.

Oak, chewing his sleeve, says something that sounds like *wah wah,* so they all clap.

"What I want to know," says Aspen, balancing her rat on her tangled hair like a toupee, "is what are we going to call him?"

"Excellent question," says MaxiMum.

"Egg *salad*," says Brian, putting them right. She's convinced that's how you say *excellent*, because eggs are her favorite; she once ate five boiled ones without throwing up.

"Granddad? Grandpa?" suggests CardaMom.

Neither of those sound remotely right.

"Iain?" says PapaDum.

"No way," moans Aspen, balancing her hoop vertically on her head and edging from side to side.

Brian makes a gigantic circle with her tiny butt, spinning the hoop twice before it drops with a clatter.

"Gramps?" says CardaMom.

Sumac shakes her head.

"*Grumps*, more like!" Pleased with this new word, Aspen does a double fist pump.

PapaDum starts a tug-of-war with Oak over the Hula-Hoop, which makes Oak laugh so much he loses his grip and topples sideways, planting his face on the mat.

✱

Up in the Artic — their art space in the attic — Sumac's working on something brilliant for Grumps. (She can't help calling him that now — just in her head, obviously, not to his face.) If dementia makes people want to talk about the past all the time, but he's too shy to start, this should help.

Then Sumac will be the first of the Lotterys that he'll warm up to during his visit, like the girl in the Narnia book — which one? — who charms the old Marsh-wiggle out of being gloomy.

So Sumac's gone through all the little faded photos in the folder labeled *Faro, Yukon, 1965–1983*, picked out the ones that show PopCorn and his parents, and laid them out on the pool table. Now she's scanning them to make a slideshow. His dead mom has a nice dimpled face, with tight curls all over her head. There's one of her in a bikini on a rock — maybe sunbathing, because there's no water nearby. And a funny one in yellow trousers and a headscarf, holding an ugly, bawling baby on her lap. Most babies are cuter than the adults they grow up to be, but with PopCorn it was clearly the opposite. Sumac uses the Ken Burns effect to zoom in slowly. Then she decides that Grumps would probably rather see his wife's pretty face than Baby PopCorn's purple one, so she changes the effect so it moves in on the mom instead. There aren't very many pictures, so Sumac makes each one last six seconds. In the old days it seems like you took a couple of pictures of your kid, then put the camera away for months until he'd grown a bit.

She tries out some cool transitions between the slides — mosaics, then droplets — but in the end she guesses an old person might prefer the pictures to come one after another like a book. For the background music, she looks up tophitsofeverydecade.com. Of the 1960s songs, she's only heard of "Wonderful World," the one with those funny lyrics about not knowing much history or biology, so she uses that, because it suits a baby.

Dangalangalong —

That's the faint ringing of the cowbell for dinner, but she's done anyway. Sumac bets the old man will be touched that she's gone to all this trouble.

Out on the Derriere (which is French for butt, because the back porch is the butt of Camelottery), there isn't enough breeze even to tinkle the chimes. "Is that rat about?" Grumps asks suspiciously.

"Aspen's not allowed to bring him to meals," Sumac assures him, "ever since he stole the ham out of MaxiMum's sandwich."

"What about a Highland grace tonight, in your dad's honor?" CardaMom says to PopCorn.

"Just the thing!" He leaps up, slaps a creepy-crawly out of the neck of his T-shirt, and launches into Scots verse:

Some have meat and cannae eat,
And some would eat that want it;
But we have meat, and we can eat,
So let the Lord be thankit!

"Booya!" Opal squawks from where he sits on the rail.

The grandfather keeps his eyes on his empty plate. Praying? Sumac wonders. Tired? Or has his brain just switched off, like a computer going into sleep mode?

PapaDum comes in from the Mess. "Sorry, the quinoa still needs another ten minutes. Brian rang the bell a bit early."

Clang-clong: Oak's invisible in a cupboard, pulling saucepans out.

"Can I do my slideshow now, then?" asks Sumac, because she'll enjoy her dinner more after it.

"Sure," says MaxiMum. "What's it about?"

"It's a surprise. For, for you," says Sumac, nodding awkwardly at the grandfather, because she still doesn't know what to call him.

"Great!" CardaMom rushes off to find the projector.

"Thoughtful kiddo," PopCorn murmurs to Sumac.

She makes sure the projector is aimed right at the big

white sheet hung up on the brick wall of the house — and gets MaxiMum to swap chairs because she's so tall she might block Grumps's view.

When everyone's settled, Sumac presses play. The song starts over an image of the Yukon mountains and the little house and old-fashioned car, with a younger Iain standing beside it in a hard hat like PapaDum used to wear on construction sites.

She sneaks a look at the old man, but she can't tell anything from his face as he sips his water.

Now comes PopCorn's mother in her polka-dot bikini, and the singer's saying he doesn't know much geography or trigonometry or algebra. There's one of her digging in the garden, with Baby PopCorn lying beside her putting his toes in his mouth —

A crash. Grumps has shoved back his chair so fast, he's almost toppled off the Derriere into the lilac bushes.

"Dad," says PopCorn, jumping up, "are you OK?"

But the old man's pushing past the kids — stepping right over Brian — and stalking into the Mess. The door thumps shut behind him.

The song's going on about one and one being two, and here's little PopCorn (still pretty ugly) riding a trike, with his mother running along behind him. . . .

Sumac turns off the slideshow with a single tap, so the big sheet on the wall is just a sheet again.

"What's up with him?" asks Aspen. "Was that from being dementored?"

PopCorn's got his hand pressed to his mouth.

Sumac's voice comes out tiny. "It was meant to be like a scrapbook."

"My bad," says CardaMom with a sigh, reaching across the table for Sumac's hand. "I said that Iain would maybe want to talk about long ago more than nowadays, but I didn't mean we should force it."

I didn't force him to do anything, Sumac thinks furiously.

"Sometimes people aren't in the mood for remembering," says PapaDum.

PopCorn picks up the almost-empty water jug and walks into the Mess.

"This is really only day one of his stay," says CardaMom. "I bet he'll warm up to us in no time."

"A stay's just another word for a visit, isn't it?" Sumac asks, her voice suddenly wobbly.

"That's . . . still under discussion," says MaxiMum, looking at PapaDum.

"We've agreed to see how it goes," he says in a not-particularly-happy voice.

Hang on. Sumac went to Yukon to help cheer the grandfather up and find him a new place to live *there*. Eleven people live in Camelottery already, just counting humans. Grumps has come for a stay with them, but it doesn't mean he can *stay*.

She slaps the laptop shut.

CHAPTER 4

- - - - - - - - - - - - - - - - - - - -

THE PRESENT

6:13 A.M. on Sumac's clock. She can hear male black-capped chickadees singing their two-note tune — *da, da* — the only birdsong she always recognizes because it's the G and F above middle C. The screen door squeals and bangs as CardaMom goes out onto the grass behind Camelottery, like she does every morning, to call out her Thanksgiving Address to the natural world. Mrs. Zhao next door sometimes gets cranky about it and puts up the radio really loud.

Then Sumac remembers about upsetting the new grandfather with her slideshow last night, when she was really trying to be nice to him. She curls up in a ball. Did he stay mad for long, she wonders? Dementia makes you forget things, which could be quite handy if the things are the kind that make you feel bad.

Above her, she can hear the bump that means Brian jumping out of bed. Why do the smallest feet always sound the loudest?

Sumac goes upstairs and through the dads' open door. "Budge up, make room," PopCorn cries.

"Sh." PapaDum beckons her into the bed, where Brian and Oak are already curled up like puppies between the dads' big bodies.

"Oak! Oaky-doke," says Brian. "Roll over!"

PapaDum shushes her.

"Oh, my dad can't expect a family this big to be quiet as the grave," says PopCorn.

"He stinky," says Brian.

"Not nice," PapaDum tells her.

"That's tobacco. I used to love the smell," says PopCorn nostalgically. He inhales Brian's shaved head. "Now you, you smell as sweet as jam."

Sumac tries a sniff of Brian. "Strawberry. No, raspberry."

"Eating jam in the night?" PopCorn asks Brian. "Out at some wild party, were you? Kicking up your heels with the Twelve Dancing Princesses?"

"I be the prince," she tells him. Brian has never actually claimed to be a boy, but she won't let anyone call her a girl either. "Where you?"

"Last night? Camping on the moon, of course."

"Nah!"

"Wood sleeps outside in the summer, doesn't he?" asks PopCorn. "Well, I sleep on the moon."

"Liar pants on fire," says Brian.

"Tickle fight!" Aspen yells from the bedroom door: She dive-bombs painfully across all five of them.

"No breaking our baby," roars Brian.

Aspen digs Oak out of the pile and holds him in the air, helicopter-style.

He giggles, his dribble a spiderweb dangling. She tilts him over PapaDum on purpose.

"Get him off!"

"I know a joke about a bed," Sumac mentions.

Aspen groans. "You kill any joke stone dead."

Sumac decides to ignore that. "Here goes. What did the blanket —"

"Everyone in the entire world knows that one," says Aspen.

Sumac presses her lips together and decides to try it another time, when her sister's not around. "Can we go to the beach today?" she asks instead.

"Why not?" says PopCorn.

"Except, if your dad —" begins PapaDum.

Argh. He'd slipped out of Sumac's mind again for a split second.

PopCorn pulls a face. "Maybe not today, then," he tells her.

Sumac wishes the old man was still in Yukon being dormant. Now he's more like a volcano that's starting to rumble.

"But very soon," says PopCorn. "We can't put our lives on hold."

"Can he still swim, with his dimension?" Aspen wonders.

"Demen*tia*," Sumac corrects her.

PopCorn giggles: "I like that: *The Grandfather from Another Dimension!* Yeah, I bet he remembers how to swim."

Something's been bothering Sumac. "He doesn't really seem like he has a brain emergency."

"Well, I suppose he's only lost some of his marbles so far, which means the gaps don't show up in every conversation," says PopCorn, tapping his head. "Like Swiss cheese — perfectly solid in between the holes."

Aspen plonks Oak onto Brian. "My turn for tickles, everybody else scoot."

"*You* scoot," growls Brian.

"Nearests and dearests," says PopCorn, squeezing all four kids in his arms, "love is not a pie."

"You mean it's not gooey?" asks Aspen.

"What other qualities does a pie have?" asks PapaDum. "Crumbly? Sticky? Foul, if it's pumpkin?"

"We don't have to fight for a slice?" suggests Sumac.

PopCorn nods. "There really is enough for everyone, because it's a magic pie that gets bigger when —" Then he lets out a terrible groan because Brian's knelt on his stomach.

✳

No beach today, because the parents are busy arranging stuff for the grandfather. CardaMom puts the sprinkler on in the afternoon, but it's not the same as lake waves.

Right now Sumac is being Milkweed Monitor at the very back of the Wild, trying to blow bugs away from her face. Bent over a randomly chosen square meter with a magnifying glass, she fills in the weekly data sheet that she'll mail to the monarch butterfly program.

Density (# of milkweed plants)	
Rainfall (past 24 hours)	
Temperature	
Larval instars	
Aphids (live/mummified)	

Sumac likes doing citizen science — like, in this case, helping figure out what the butterflies need if they're going to survive — but she's got sunscreen melting into her eyes, and they're stinging so much she can hardly tell a blob of monarch latex from an egg. She'd actually rather be reading *Ballet Shoes* on her belly in the Tree Fort, where she could smell the cut grass but stay out of the sun.

When she finally staggers back up the yard, wondering if she has sunstroke maybe, she finds CardaMom — yellow pollen all down her braid — weeding the boat-shaped raised beds of lettuces. Brian, in nothing but tiny swim shorts and a plastic medieval breastplate, is helping her. Opal's by his portable perch in the sunshine, picking ants out of the grass, and Topaz is writhing pleasurably on her back on the cover of the Hot Tub. (The cats don't seem to think of Opal as a real bird they should try to eat, which is a bit insulting, Sumac thinks.)

Oak crawls over to Sumac, ghah-ghahing, suspiciously brown around the mouth. "Have you been eating dirt again, Oaky-doke?"

He grins radiantly.

"Not again!" CardaMom straightens, pressing the arch of her back, and scoops him up. "Full speed ahead to the OK Corral. . . ."

That's Oak's plastic play yard, parked in the shade of the big maple. She deposits him in there with a stack of old flowerpots and a beach ball.

"Come and get hydrated, kids." PapaDum walks out of the house with a jug of lemonade, a platter of yellow watermelon under a mesh cover, and muffins that are still steaming. They're banana, tinted pink with beet juice, and PapaDum's probably snuck lots of ground-up seeds into them, but you can't tell.

Aspen inserts one in each cheek and mumbles, "Look, I'm a chipmunk."

Sumac spots MaxiMum down the back of the Wild in rubber boots, gloves, and a white mask, like something out of an end-of-the-world movie. "What are you doing?" she calls.

"Collecting raccoon droppings so we don't pick up parasitic worms that'll make us go blind or fall into a coma."

"Ew," says Sumac. Droppings: there's another euphemism. Excrement, feces, scat, dung, or guano if you're a bird.

CardaMom brings over a slice of watermelon and lifts MaxiMum's mask to feed it to her.

Just then Aspen shrieks from the house: "My back!"

Has she shot herself with a Nerf gun at really close range again? (In the back, is that possible?) Or was she playing the totally forbidden Tightrope Walk on the Banisters and she's fallen down four flights of stairs?

No. "They're back," that's what she's shrieking. And Diamond's barking crazily, which means it's the dog's beloved Wood and the other two big sibs, home from Camp Jagged Falls at last.

Sic's Afro is huger than ever, with pine needles in it, and his old T-shirt is one of the first he ever printed: *Free Shrugs*, a pun on *Free Hugs*. Aspen pushes past Sumac to jump on his back like a vampire bat and kiss his ear.

"Smackeroo," Sic cries next, opening his arms at Sumac.

He's the only one who calls her that. She gives him the longest hug and whispers in his ear: "I missed you nearly as much as I didn't miss Catalpa."

That makes him laugh.

Wood follows, barefoot, scratched, and burr-studded as usual, Diamond panting at his heel. You'd hardly notice she only has three legs unless you knew to look.

"You're fuzzy," Sumac tells Sic.

Her big brother grins, rubbing his stubbly cheeks. "Hard to shave in the backcountry. . . ."

Wood, jealous, mimes machine-gunning him.

"One of these years you too will have facial hair, little man," Sic tells him, slapping his back, then ducking away from Wood's fist. Even though Wood's only twelve, his punches are the hardest.

"We should have tied you up and left you in the bush for the coyotes to eat," says Wood, as deep-voiced as he can.

"Is that any way to talk to your Team Leader?"

"You only got picked for that because of age discrimination." Wood is glowering. "It should be based on knowledge — like, wood lore."

"Wood lore?" Catalpa yelps with laughter as she heads out of the Mess. "You total hobbit." She runs straight to Oak, hoisting him out of his corral to kiss him all over. She's covered in angry-looking mosquito bites, Sumac notices.

"Why you all spotty?" Brian asks Catalpa.

"Because bugs find her delicious, and who can blame them?" says CardaMom, arms wrapped around her teenagers in a double hug that's halfway to a wrestle.

Sumac's secretly relieved that it'll be three years before she has to go on the wilderness trip and spend two weeks living off trail mix, jerky, and rehydrated chili. She tries to think of something friendly to say to her biggest sister, who hasn't even said hi yet. "Hey, I like your friendship bracelets." They go right up Catalpa's golden arm; some of them have beads in them, and even leaves and tiny feathers in resin. "Do you actually remember who made each one?"

"I could never forget," says Catalpa. (Dramatically, the way she says everything these days.) She names them: "Madison, Addison, Ashley, Olivia, Mackenzie, Maya, Alexis, Jazmyn, other Madison . . ."

"Me and Aspen have been making friendship bracelets too, out of old Rainbow Loom bands," Sumac tells her.

Catalpa shakes her head. "They're not proper friendship bracelets unless they're thread."

Sumac chews her lip and wishes her sister had stayed away a bit longer.

"We gots another grandfather," Brian announces, pointing.

And Sumac's stomach sinks, because she'd actually forgotten. They all spin around, and there's PopCorn leading his unsmiling father out into the Wild.

CardaMom makes all the introductions. Grumps's drippy eyes shift from face to face, and it's one of those moments when Sumac sees her family as if from outer space. *What a lot of us.* Is it scary to meet a whole gang of new grandchildren all at the same time, she wonders?

Grumps doesn't look scared, just grim as ever.

Sic is charming, of course, as if he's been waiting to meet his fourth grandfather all his sixteen years of life.

Wood just nods, all tough-guy as usual.

Catalpa produces a minimal wave. "Can I —" She nods upward toward her Turret. "I promised the band we'd jam."

"Since when are you in a band?" scoffs Wood.

Oh, great, thinks Sumac. That's all Catalpa needs to turn her into a complete monster.

"It's a virtual one called Game of Tones," says Catalpa, "and Mackenzie's pretty sure the others will vote me in once I upload a sample track."

The stubbled ridges on the old man's forehead soar. "What's a virtual band when it's at home?"

"Ah, each of us, we're going to record to a click track, and once the piece is collaboratively mastered we'll release it virally, you know?"

Sumac doesn't think the grandfather understood any of that.

"So you're just teenagers messing around online," Wood spells out.

"That's a drastic oversimplification," says Catalpa, glaring at her brother.

"Game of Drones, I like it," says Sic.

"Tones," Catalpa corrects him.

He keeps a straight face but winks at Sumac.

Sic's been trying to teach her to wink for years, but it makes half her face scrunch up, and then Aspen always asks her (fake concerned) if she's having a stroke.

✳

The Lotterys are walking to dinner. They pass a cyclist who's arguing furiously with a taxi driver. Then they cut through some kind of pop-up street fair called Fruitarama. A century and a half ago, when the huge redbrick houses like Camelottery were built, the neighborhood used to be the city's richest. Then an expressway cut it off from the lake, and it turned into the poorest. Now it's what PopCorn calls a mixed bag, which makes things interesting.

After CardaMom's class — she "volun-teaches" kids who can't afford voice and violin lessons — she's coming to meet the family at Pete's Rear, which is how Brian once misheard their local pizzeria. It looks really narrow and scuzzy at the front, but at the back there's a vast patio strung with fairy lights and a table big enough for the Lotterys.

Though tonight there's only actually ten of them, because PopCorn and his dad have stayed home to eat something called bangers and mash.

The first quarter of an hour is mostly chat about canoeing and portaging and tumplines, though it's hard to make out every detail through the teenagers' facefuls of pizza. Oak manages to wrap his fingers around one of the mini triangles and cram his whole fist into his mouth. Tomato sauce leaks out like fake blood.

"So, about my learning to drive," says Sic, shooting out a deft arm to take a fourth slice and fold it on the way to his mouth.

"Not this again," groans PapaDum.

CardaMom takes Sic's stubbly cheeks between her hands. "Firstborn. We don't have a car."

"Aha. Glad you raised that," says Sic, "because there's a 1992 Camry with a slightly cracked windshield on Autotrader going for a mere three hundred and fifty bucks."

"Sounds like a chick magnet all right," says Catalpa mockingly.

"The technical term would be a lemon," says PapaDum.

Aspen, who finds food a chore, has eaten the dry crust of her slice, picked the cheese off and made a ball of it, and abandoned the rest.

Sic's still smiling. "But with a bit of luck . . ."

"We've used up all our luck with the lottery and you lot." CardaMom's shaking her head so hard, her braid is a jumping snake. "The universe doesn't owe this family another thing."

Oak has a piece of pizza pasted to his round cheek, Sumac notices.

"Besides," says MaxiMum, "we don't have a parking space for a hypothetical car."

"We could convert the Hoopla back into one," suggests Sic.

"No way!"

All three parents shush Wood as Luigi (their favorite waiter) frowns across the patio.

The Hoopla's the space in front of Camelottery that used to be for parking. When the moms and dads first moved in, they tried to rewild it with native plants, but it was always scruffy with broken bottles and the pee of passersby. As soon as Wood could talk, he successfully campaigned for concrete and a basketball hoop instead.

"Convert your room into a compost heap," Wood throws in Sic's direction.

Aspen snorts with laughter. She's practicing bending her thumbs back now; Sumac can't look.

"Anyway," says PapaDum, "there's something important we have to talk about."

"Gelato," says Wood, "that's important."

"Vanilla," cries Brian. "Vanilla, Oaky-doke!"

Oak squeaks with excitement.

"Could I have blood orange, passion fruit, *and* stracciatella, because it's been a whole month since I've tasted anything in the frozen dessert line?" asks Sic.

That sounds to Sumac like a disgusting combination, but her big brother was born experimental.

MaxiMum nods, trying to catch Luigi's eye while she cleans Oak up with a wet wipe.

"So why didn't the old codger come along tonight, doesn't he like pizza?" asks Wood.

Us, Sumac thinks, her throat tightening as she swallows the last of her crust. It's us he doesn't like.

The parents exchange a slow, three-way look. "Actually, Iain is what — who — we need to talk about," says PapaDum, putting his knife and fork together neatly.

"How long's he here for?" asks Catalpa. "Because I told Olivia and Mackenzie and Celize they could come anytime this summer."

"Ah, possible problem. I said the same to Baruch and Ben-Zion," says Sic.

Sumac remembers to ask, "Can I have Isabella over for a double sleepover this weekend, with hot dogs?"

"Camp behind the house, softies," Wood tells his siblings scornfully.

"Listen," says MaxiMum, "no visitors till further notice. It looks like your grandfather's going to live with us for the moment."

Goggle eyes all round, except for Aspen, who's preoccupied with trying to tie three of her fingers in a knot.

Catalpa asks what Sumac would have asked if she could control her voice: "*The moment*, what does that mean?"

"For the present," says CardaMom, making a wobbling gesture with her hand, "depending on how it goes."

"He not a present," says Brian mutinously.

Sic's the first to recover. "Well, this should be good for a few laughs. Does he have a car?"

"Give it a rest!" That's Wood.

"Not one he'll be bringing all the way from Yukon," says PapaDum.

"But Camelottery's ours!" Catalpa shakes back her black hair like a rock star. "You can't just ship in some random old guy behind our backs the minute we're out of contact range."

For once, Sumac finds herself in total agreement with her big sister, which feels odd.

"He's PopCorn's *dad*," CardaMom reminds them.

"The fact is, Iain doesn't seem to be safe driving or living on his own anymore," says PapaDum.

"And he's got nowhere else to go," adds CardaMom.

MaxiMum raises one elegant eyebrow.

"Well — nowhere else that —" CardaMom hesitates. "I mean, of course there are homes, but . . ."

"Places where he very well might be happier," murmurs MaxiMum.

"Isn't Camelottery a home?" Sumac asks, puzzled.

"She means, like, orphanages for oldies," Wood tells her.

"Yeah, we could pay for him to be looked after by strangers," says CardaMom, "but luckily we have enough folks and time and room to take him in, so we've decided to try this first."

"Luckily?" echoes Catalpa, as if she's about to be sick. "We haven't even had a Fleeting." That's Lottery for a family meeting. "Call this a democracy!"

"It's not, *tsi't-ha*, it's a family," says CardaMom.

"Sometimes," says MaxiMum, "as the parents, it's our job —"

"The Council of Four has spoken," Sic interrupts in a sinister video-game voice.

"I'm afraid this is a like-it-or-lump-it situation," says PapaDum.

"Come on, kids," says CardaMom, "let's open our hearts. *There's room for another, said Mrs. —*" She breaks off. "Macroom? McCrone?"

"Huh?" says Wood.

"Some old song."

Sumac should look it up for CardaMom. She's the Lotterys' good girl, the practical one, the helper, the one who solves problems instead of causing them. Isn't she?

And Oak starts to wail, because he's rubbed pizza sauce into his eye.

CHAPTER 5

ROOM FOR ANOTHER

The next morning, Sumac's in ancient Sumer. Well, actually, in her room sitting right against the vent with a tablet. (Every summer, PapaDum resists putting on the air-conditioning because it guzzles so much power and hurts the planet, but he cracked a week ago and turned it up high.) She's researching magic spells, boastful inscriptions, weird recipes, poems by Enheduanna — priestess of Ur — who may have been the first writer ever. . . . *Dumu* looks like dummy but actually means child. To call someone a dummy you say *ludima*, which Sumac remembers because it's like ludicrous.

"Busy?" MaxiMum leans in around the door.

"My head's too full," says Sumac, "like my tummy after too much pie."

"So, about Iain. We've been talking about where would be best for him."

Aha. Maybe the parents have slept on it and realized that Camelottery's not right for him after all?

"We're thinking ground floor, so he'll have a bathroom close by, and no stairs and baby gates to deal with."

Sumac keeps her face blank to hide her disappointment.

"I thought you'd understand. You're such a rational being." MaxiMum bends to kiss the part in her hair.

MaxiMum doesn't kiss the kids very often, so it's worth at least double when she does. Also, *rational* is her highest compliment because it means your brain works logically.

"OK, then. We're assuming you'd prefer Spare Oom to the Overspill in the basement? I'll —"

MaxiMum breaks off as a squawk goes up in the Hall of Mirrors outside the door: "Somebody!" (That's how Brian calls for help, because there are so many Lotterys. Not that Brian admits to needing help very often.)

Hang on a second, thinks Sumac. What was that about preferring Spare Oom?

But MaxiMum's gone, leaving Sumac pop-eyed with outrage. *Ground floor. Bathroom close by.* That means *this* room, *her* room. The one that's had the sign on the door —

Sumac's Room, with a picture of a red, flame-shaped sumac berry cluster — since she was one day old. Do the dads and moms seriously expect her to give it up?

Rational, my butt! She kicks her beanbag, almost hoping to send polystyrene peas snow-showering all over the room, but instead her foot skids off and she stubs it on the leg of her desk.

Curled up on the floor, Sumac sobs as she rubs her toe, which is probably broken. She'll have to wear a cast, and then she won't be able to manage stairs and baby gates either, and they'll have to let her stay in this room instead of banishing her three flights up to spidery old Spare Oom.

When Sumac emerges, it's with her sheets and pillows wrapped up in her rainbow-striped duvet, a bad limp, and a story that's nearly true. When asked what happened to her foot, she's going to say she hurt it moving all her stuff because of having to sacrifice her room to the new grandfather.

She manages to open the first baby gate, but shutting it — without getting sheets caught in the hinges — is the problem. She hobbles up to the second floor and blows crossly up at the mobile of the solar system, making Jupiter bang into Saturn. Not a peep from the moms' room, or the dads'. No sound from behind the sign in Brian's scrawl, with half the letters backward:

⎰ 8riAu + oA ʞ ≥9≥ Яum
⎱ 9v8udY 9I≥ C99p oT9 !!!

Sumac's foot still hurts. But she stops limping, because there's no point unless someone's there to see.

A terrible thumping up on the landing. Sumac heaves her bedding over the next gate, then climbs over, trampling the sheets with her dusty sandals.

"Why are you pogoing?" she asks her red-faced oldest brother.

"This is just" — thunk — "a brief interval" — thunk, thunk — "in my strawberry training."

"Your what?"

Sic pulls the plastic strawberry kitchen timer out of his pocket. "It's a thing." Thunk, thunk, thunk, he goes on his pogo stick. "Brainwork for twenty minutes, recap for two, then take a four-minute break and get your pulse up."

Today's silkscreened T-shirt says *Bad Spellers of the World, Untie!* "But why are you pogoing *inside?*" Sumac asks.

"Because it's disgustingly hot out there."

PapaDum puts his head out of the Loud Lounge. "Son, you're going to smash the floor."

"It's a calculated risk, and I've calculated that it's unlikely," Sic assures him. "These boards have stood up to a lot of punishment since 1884."

Oak squeals, so PapaDum disappears back inside without a word to Sumac about her trailing roll of bedding. She sniffs, rage building up again.

"What about you, what are you up to?" Sic asks.

At last, someone's asking. "Well, I *was* studying Sumerian —"

Most people would laugh or not believe her, but her brother nods. "I went on an Elvish kick when I was nine. What can you say so far?"

"Mostly insults." Sumac puts on a gravelly voice: "*Nuzu egalla bacar!* That's a proverb that means *Ignoramuses are numerous in the palace.*"

Sic sniggers. "I like it! A laid-back way of calling the people you live with idiots."

"Yeah," says Sumac, "like, as it happens, right now, all the parents are being —"

And she's about to tell the whole story about being forced practically at gunpoint to move out of her own lovely blue-sky-room-since-she-was-born, but the strawberry in Sic's hand buzzes, and he swings the pogo stick over his shoulder like a battle-weary soldier with his rifle and heads back to his room.

"What's your next strawberry?" she asks.

"Regulatory, Warning, Temporary Conditions, and Information and Direction Signs."

Sumac frowns in puzzlement. And only figures it out after he's disappeared behind the door marked *Sic Planet*, which has a funny cartoon Catalpa did for him of the earth looking nauseous. In spite of the dads and moms quashing the idea last night, Sic must be learning to drive.

She wonders if Sumerians put up clay signs to direct cart traffic through the cities of Uruk or Ur.

She needs somebody else to gripe to. The door of the Wood Cabin hangs open. (It's wallpapered to look like bare boards — a visual pun on her brother's name.) Wood's probably in the Ravine, with Diamond on a leash so she won't chase or trample anything.

The door to Catalpa's Turret — painted to trick the eye into thinking that it's ancient iron — is shut too. Oh yeah, Catalpa's off feeding and playing with her guide dogs in training. She even cleans out their kennels, which she says is yuck but not as much as diapers. Catalpa hates volunteering unless it involves animals, so if it wasn't for the dogs she'd probably be spending all of July flat on her bed rereading her Tamora Pierce and Suzanne Collins novels.

Nobody's here to be interested in why Sumac's toiling up to the attic under a gigantic ball of bedding.

Up to the attic she goes. Grumps's possessions are out of Spare Oom already — his cases standing zipped up on the landing — but the room's still cramped, crammed with boxes of the Lotterys' junk. A dark curtain blocks out one miserable window. A rowing machine leans against one wall, metal arms out to grab Sumac. The ceiling slants right over the bed, so she'll probably bang her head on it when she sits up in the night all confused about where she is. (Then she'll need to stumble down to the third floor for the toilet, in the dark, with a concussion, probably, as well as her broken toe.) This is more of a bat roost than a bedroom. How can the parents, how dare they —

Sumac makes the bed, wearing a fixed scowl. Her sheets don't seem to fit right; she wrenches at the corner so hard, she hears something rip. She puts boxes out onto the landing, stacking them up to form a barricade. The closet rail falls down as soon as she touches it, and wire hangers jangle in a big tangly mess.

She stomps up and down through Camelottery three times, leaving all the gates open, because she has to haul her stuff to the attic in garbage bags, and she can't do that and keep Oak safe too, and nobody even comes out and asks what she's doing and can they help her with that!

Sumac tosses her clothes into the stiff drawers of the old dresser. No point in being tidy, because this room's never going to look nice anyway. She shoves her corkboard and blackboard into the dusty space under the bed. Same goes for her rolled-up fluffy white rug. She crams her books onto the shelves any which way, in a double layer because there isn't enough room. She dumps her dolls in a bag at the back of the closet, because there's nowhere to display them. She tosses the *Sumac's Room* sign on top; she's not going to nail it up on the door, because it isn't true.

On her last trip to the room she's lived in for nine years, Sumac gives it a sorrowful glance. She yanks her gauze canopy out of the ceiling, and she doesn't bother picking up the nail that rolls away across the floor. Bare, the room looks weird now: a prison cell muraled with a summer sky.

Up on the third floor, limping into the Loud Lounge, Sumac collapses in a swivel chair.

Nobody asks why she seems too tired to speak. Aspen's playfighting with her rat on a big cushion. CardaMom and PapaDum are in the middle of a game of Slo-Mo Catch with Oak, who's hiccuping with mirth. Then they put him down beside the sofa, so he can practice pulling himself up and cruising around it.

"How's your new room?" asks CardaMom, putting her hand on Sumac's neck. "Sumac's being extraordinarily generous and giving your grandfather her bedroom," she tells the others.

Which makes Sumac kind of want to spit, because how can she burst out complaining now?

Aspen's jaw drops. "How come?"

"The guy's eighty-two years old," snaps Sumac. "He can't be expected to climb all the way up to the attic every time he wants a pair of socks." Trying to sound noble, but it comes out more like haughty.

PapaDum stands up. "Shall we get started on moving your stuff upstairs, hon?"

"Actually, I've done it all." Her voice wobbles a little with a mixture of self-pity and pride.

"What a star," cries CardaMom.

"Anything need fixing?" PapaDum asks.

"Lots of things," says Sumac, thinking about the rail in the closet, for starters.

MaxiMum puts her head in the door. "Sumac, I've cleaned your window, baseboards, and floor, so it's looking brighter, at least. If somebody can help me shift that old rowing machine and bring in another bookcase —"

"On it," says PapaDum.

And Sumac feels even worse, because she wants to hug her parents and kick them in the butts at the same time.

✱

Twelve for brunch, and Sumac has no elbow room at all. Aspen bounces up and down on her ball right opposite her, then braces her hands on the table and bends her elbows so far forward that they touch, like some giant spider.

Sumac looks away from her mutant sister and pours a careful trickle of maple syrup on her stack of pancakes.

"Doing OK this morning, Iain?" CardaMom puts her hand on the sleeve of Grumps's long flannel shirt. "It must all be a bit overwhelming, after your nice, quiet little house."

He stares at his plate as if he hasn't heard her.

"Bet it's a tad hotter than you're used to as well," says Sic.

"We get all weathers in Faro." A heavy pause. "Are there no pancakes except the speckledy kind?"

"They're thirteen-grain, really delicious," CardaMom assures him.

"Plus, they keep you regular," jokes Sic.

The old man gives him a baleful stare.

PapaDum sets down a huge platter of bacon.

"I was under the impression your kind never touched pig," says Grumps.

PapaDum tilts his head to one side. "Are you thinking of Muslims, maybe?"

"Orthodox Jews?" suggests Sic.

A shrug from Grumps.

"I was raised Hindu," says PapaDum, "and my parents don't eat meat, but as it happens, I'm an omnivore."

Grumps points at his son's plate. "Anyway, I thought *you* were a vegetarian." He pronounces it like a foreign word.

"What can I say, Dad? I can't live without the very occasional, humanely raised, crispy rasher." PopCorn folds another slide of bacon into his mouth. *"Do I contradict myself?"* he goes on in what Sumac recognizes as his poetry voice. *"Very well, then, I contradict myself! I am large, I contain multitudes . . ."*

"You'll be large, all right, if you carry on stuffing your face like that," says Grumps.

PopCorn closes his eyes briefly, then chews on.

Sumac realizes something: This old man probably made up his mind to hate it at Camelottery before he even walked in the door.

Aspen slurps the bottom of her protein shake noisily and leaps off her ball.

"Take a Lot before you go." MaxiMum holds out the old top hat. (The Lotterys used to put their Lots in a Tibetan singing bowl, but the hat is way more Hogwarts.)

"I'm going to give Slate a sponge bath after just-super-quickly-checking if anyone's attacked my portal. He's horribly sweaty." Aspen takes Slate out of her hoodie pocket and scratches his white belly. He plants one of his nibbly kisses on her chin.

"Bathing him doesn't count as housework," says Sumac, "because he's your rat, and it's fun."

"And no screen time till you're done, Aspen, no matter what state your portal's in," says MaxiMum, shaking the hat till Aspen takes a Lot.

"Drop Everything and Read." Aspen scowls at her card. "CardaMom, trade?"

"You don't even know what I've got," CardaMom points out as she plucks a Lot out of the hat.

Aspen yanks it out of her hand. *"Fill a Toy Basket.* Deal!"

"I get to drop everything and read *The Orenda!"* CardaMom punches the air in satisfaction.

"And don't fill the basket with just one big cuddly," PapaDum warns Aspen.

PopCorn is scanning the listings in the city freesheet. *"Bambini,* who wants to come hear an Australian aboriginal country-and-western singer-songwriter tonight?"

Sic looks over his shoulder and pokes the page. "There's a postpunk hip-hop crew in the mainspace, I'd go to that while you're upstairs with the folkies."

"That works."

"Cat Girl?" asks Sic.

Catalpa's only just come downstairs in her long black nightshirt. "Unless I'm out crochet-tagging," she yawns.

She and a bunch of other fourteen-year-olds are currently obsessed with making colorful patches to cover bike stands and pipes and park benches. Like graffiti but with yarn.

"And for your challenge," says PopCorn, "you can each review it on the family blog."

Sumac goes to take just one more piece of bacon. . . .

But Grumps is already eating the last one. His jaw moves like he's not even enjoying it.

Wood dumps everything compostable in the metal bucket and sets down the rest on a plate for Diamond. CardaMom's scrubbing the grill pan; she flicks her braid out of the scummy water. MaxiMum puts three pills beside Grumps's plate.

"That stuff's not doing a thing for me," he says.

"Mm," she says, "the doctor said they take a few weeks to kick in."

"Giving me bad dreams."

"I'm sorry about that, Iain. The side effects usually fade with time."

"Hard on the stomach too."

"If you take them after a meal, like right now," says MaxiMum, "that should help."

102

Finally, he sticks out his lizard tongue and swallows them. (MaxiMum's so persistent, it occurs to Sumac, she could probably talk anyone into jumping off a cliff.)

"Kapow!" shrieks Opal from his perch.

Grumps glares over his shoulder at the bird.

"You likes parrots?" Brian asks him.

A sniff. "In their place."

She looks confused. "Opal gots lots of places."

"I was thinking of the jungle. How do ye manage?"

"Manage?" repeats MaxiMum.

"Hygienically." His red-and-purple nose wrinkles. "With it flapping hither and yon and dropping its whatsits."

"Oh, Opal doesn't fly," says PapaDum.

"And don't worry, PapaDum's trained him to go on a sheet of paper on that shelf there," says MaxiMum.

"PapaDum's Opal's flock leader, that's like the alpha dog," Wood explains.

"See his squinchy wing?" Aspen jumps up to stroke the left one. "He got smuggled in a suitcase and it damaged him. We're his rescue family."

"Something wrong with all of them?" asks Grumps.

The Lotterys stare at him.

He nods at Diamond, lying on her cushion near Wood. "That crippled mutt, and the cat who's scared of his own shadow. . . ."

"Quartz is a she, and she's just not as sociable as her sister, Topaz," says Sumac, "but there's nothing wrong with being an introvert."

"And if you bothered to actually watch Diamond," says Wood, "she moves better on three legs than most dogs do on four."

A leaden silence. Two days, thinks Sumac; the grandfather's only been here since the evening before last, but he's like a gray thundercloud hovering over the house.

The old man plonks his plate beside the sink.

"Does Grumps not have to pick a Lot? Is he too old for chores?" Aspen asks.

Sumac glares dragon fire at her sister. He's not meant to know what they call him.

"What did you say?" he demands.

"Nothing," says Aspen weakly.

MaxiMum and CardaMom are exchanging a look.

"*Grumps*, you said, I heard you."

"It's kind of like Gramps, you know, grandfather," says Sumac.

"It is not. A grump is a cranky puss," says the old man.

He leaves the Mess without another word. And without anyone asking him to take a Lot, Sumac notices. Clearly he's going to be like the king and the rest of them are the servants.

The parents don't comment.

After a minute, PapaDum picks *File Paperwork*, but he says that's so tedious and swaps it for PopCorn's *Hang Laundry on the Clotheslines*. MaxiMum says she'll keep *Weed Veggie Beds*. (More of a pleasure than a job, for her.)

Brian gets to choose a green card (which means an easy one), and Sumac reads it for her: *"Fill Birdbaths."*

Brian nods importantly. "What for Oak?"

"Ah . . ." Oak's not really old enough to be a lot of use yet, but Brian insists on including her little brother in everything, so Sumac offers him the hat. Oak seizes a fist-ful of cards. She extracts a green one from his sticky grip. It actually says *Clear the Floor of Your Bedroom*, but she thinks for a second, then says, *"Dance,"* because that's one of his talents.

"Want to dance, Oaky?" asks Brian. "Dance?"

He jolts up and down in his high chair and lets out a high-pitched shriek.

Lastly, Sumac draws a card of her own. *"Clean Toilets,"* she reads aloud in a tone of woe. "All four, seriously?"

CardaMom's a soft touch. "You start on the third floor, me in the basement," she offers, "and I'll race you to the second floor."

MaxiMum's rinsing plates with one hand and stacking them in the nearer dishwasher with the other. "And listen, kids, we all have to be more responsible about picking up things off the ground."

"Especially on the stairs," says PapaDum. "I just read that households with young children have the highest rate of falls, but the family members most likely to be hurt are those over sixty-five, because their bones are more brittle."

Sumac thinks of peanut brittle going snap. If Grumps had to go to the hospital, would she get her room back? She wonders how long people live after eighty-two, then feels terrible and tries to forget she even thought it.

✷

Passing the door of her old room, Sumac hears MaxiMum inside. "This was Sumac's room, but we can repaint it however you'd prefer, Iain, it's no trouble."

They're going to paint over the mural that PopCorn did for her when she was five?

"Sumac. Is she the gorgeous one?" she hears Grumps asking.

Sumac grits her teeth. He's thinking of Catalpa. He could at least say something like, *How kind of her to lend me her lovely bedroom.*

"I find all our children gorgeous," says MaxiMum. "Sumac's very precise, thoughtful, responsible. . . ."

She'd usually be glad to hear this, but right now they sound like dog qualities, and she'd swap all of them for one *gorgeous*.

"She's the wee oriental, then? Or is she an Indian like Cardigan, whatshername, the other lady?"

He means CardaMom. So Grumps is one of those white people who describe everybody-whose-skin-isn't-exactly-like-theirs as if they're another species.

Instead of answering, MaxiMum says, pleasantly, "You've got a multicolored family now, Iain."

"Like a bag of Smarties," he says. And not as if he's a big fan of Smarties. "Who are you to my son again?"

Can he have forgotten, Sumac wonders? Is this a lost marble? Or is he just being rude?

"Friend for twenty years, coparent of seven kids," says MaxiMum.

Talking to this man is a sort of obstacle course for not losing your temper, Sumac decides. Well, he's met his match in MaxiMum.

Sumac peeks into her poor abandoned room. Two cases stand beside the chair like guards. Maybe one of the brain marbles Grumps is missing is how to unpack a bag? She notices her five-by-five Rubik's Cube in the corner, behind him, and she wants to retrieve it but doesn't dare.

"See, *kunuk* is ancient Sumerian for seal," Sumac tells Isabella, "and for more than one of something they just stuck *.ene* on the end, so these are *kunuk.ene.*" They're in the Mess making clay seals to bake in the stove. Isabella and Sumac are doing cylinder seals like the Mesopotamians wore on strings around their wrists so if they wanted to seal something quickly they could just roll the picture on.

"Remind me why you're trying to learn this language if everyone who ever spoke it is dead?" asks her friend, folding up the sleeves of her dress twice before she picks up the steak knife. Today Isabella's nails are emerald green.

"Why not?" says Sumac with a shrug. "It's all brain-ercise. Next time someone assumes I was adopted from China and asks me am I taking Mandarin classes, I can gobsmack them by saying, *No, actually, Sumerian.*"

"Ha! What are you carving — fairies?"

"Duh, it's a banquet scene," says Sumac. "There's PapaDum with his big beard, see? And the rest of us, all the way down to Oak crawling. I was going to arrange us by height, with MaxiMum first, but then I decided that in ancient times people would have been more impressed by age, because you had to be pretty clever or lucky to live long."

"Mine's going to be all flowers," says Isabella, cutting into the clay.

Aspen feels her way into the Mess, blindfolded with a long sock. (She's studying the senses with MaxiMum by doing without one of them at a time.) When she bangs her head on a cupboard, she pulls the sock off. "Hey, I want to do one of them."

Sumac represses a sigh and cuts her sister a slice from the clay block.

"Why isn't PopCorn helping us?" Isabella complains.

He usually does, with art, not to mention the fact that Mesopotamia was meant to be his and Sumac's special Lottafun . . . but Sumac supposes that's gone down the tubes. "He's taking his dad to a Center for Geriatric Neurology," she grumbles.

"What's that?" asks Isabella.

"Somewhere old people get tested, like old cars."

"I bet they diagnose him with terminal crabbypantsitis," jokes Aspen.

"He keeps talking as if PapaDum's just arrived from India instead of having been here since he was eleven. And he's rude about the food. He peered into the salad PapaDum was making this morning like he was looking for worms," Sumac tells her friend, "and then he said, *Not my cup of tea.*"

"Is there weird stuff in the salad, though?"

"Well, goat cheese, beets, arugula," says Sumac, "a bit of freekeh."

Isabella's lip curls up. "What the freak is freekeh?"

"A supergrain, nuttyish."

Isabella pretends to retch. "What I'm curious about is, will his eyebrows ever grow back?"

"I doubt it," says Sumac with a shrug. "Your cells aren't as growy when you're old."

Aspen's cut herself a much thicker chunk of clay, and she's making a cylinder like a can of beans. Her rat looks out from the pocket of her pajamas.

"Slate," Sumac scolds him, "are you responsible for all those gouges and scratches?"

"That's my carving," says Aspen.

"What's it meant to be?" asks Isabella, leaning so close that her braids almost touch it.

"Just abstract, like Jackson Pollock," Aspen says smugly.

She always says Jackson Pollock when she can't be bothered doing proper art, because he's famous for putting his canvases on the floor and splatting paint all over them. And she gets away with it, because if you use words like *proper art* at Camelottery, PopCorn says, *Proper, plopper, it's all about the journey.*

"Cool idea, though, Sumac, to let him help," Aspen

adds, setting Slate on the table and pressing one of his tiny paws onto the clay.

"Put him away!" Isabella's stepped back, shuddering.

Aspen gives Sumac a your-pal's-pathetic look.

Sumac scowls back at her. Isabella may be a bit of a cowardy custard, but at least she doesn't do armpit farts like that boy Aspen keeps bringing home.

Sumac keeps picking at her banqueting figures, but she's only making them worse. Art's not one of her fortes. And grrr, *THE LOTTERYS* should be in mirror writing to make the words come out right when she uses the seal! She can't seem to concentrate today. She smears the letters with her knife and starts rewriting them.

Now Wood walks in barefoot and slaps down a wet pike as long as his arm.

"*Hola*, Wood," says Isabella, giving him a finger wave.

He barely nods as he takes his pocketknife to the fish and scrapes out its guts.

Isabella's all agog. "Did you seriously just catch that?"

"Yeah. Cloudy mornings are ideal, because the fish don't go deep to avoid the sun."

Sumac suspects her best friend of *liking* Wood, but she's never asked, because she doesn't want to know.

"So hey, I hear you're being an Environmental Steward this summer, is that as important as it sounds?" asks Isabella.

"It's mostly mulching plants," mutters Sumac.

"Mulching is crucial," says Wood.

Isabella lays her head on the counter, to look the fish in the eye, while Wood stuffs it with apple slices that keep sliding back out. "Ugly bugly!"

"By pike standards, you're hideous," he points out.

She lets out an outraged gasp.

"Flat nose, tiny mouth, no spots or shine . . ."

Isabella flounces off and examines the little plastic bags held to the refrigerator by magnets. "Wood, June 22 . . . Diamond, July 13 . . . Wood, July 13 . . ."

"They're his tick collection," explains Aspen, stabbing her thumbnails into the clay.

Wood goes to the refrigerator, and with one fish-bloody finger he points out the tiny brown bug in one bag. "All the ones that have bit me or my dog this summer."

"Have *bitten*," Sumac corrects him.

He ignores that. "I yank them out with a tweezers," he tells Isabella, "keep them to show the doctor in case I develop symptoms of, like, Lyme disease, encephalitis, that kind of thing."

"That's the most disgusting thing I've ever heard," Isabella marvels. She starts lining up the finger-puppet magnets in pairs. "Who's the new girl with the scarf?"

"Frida somebody, a painter who got literally *speared* on the handrail of a bus," says Aspen with relish, thumping her seal onto the baking sheet.

"I'll put her with . . . Sherlock Holmes," says Isabella. "And Mr. Mandela, who would you like to dance with today? Let's say . . . Jane Austen."

That makes Sumac hoot.

Isabella comes over to look at Sumac's cylinder. "Shouldn't you add your grandfather to the banquet, though, so he doesn't feel left out?"

Wood doesn't say anything. Nor Aspen, for once.

"There's no more room," says Sumac through her teeth.

CHAPTER 6

GUIDE DOG

At dinner on the Derriere, the Lotterys who went wreck diving can't talk about anything but the *Sligo*. Wood's sulking that he didn't get to go because the wreck was twenty-one meters down, and he hasn't gotten his Junior Advanced Open Water certification yet.

"It's a triple-masted schooner from 1860," Sic tells their grandfather, "with a nearly intact hull. We saw its actual stove and wheel!"

No answer from the old man. Maybe he's a bit deaf? By the time you're eighty-two, Sumac figures, bits of you must be worn out.

"It was deeply mysterious," says Catalpa, "apart from

dumb divers swarming all over it and posing for selfies."
She's wearing so much eyeliner this evening, she looks
damaged.

"Deeply," repeats Aspen with a snigger. "The shipwreck
at the bottom of the lake was *deeply* mysterious! Get it?"

Catalpa closes her eyes for a second, which is code for
Somebody take this child away before I smack her.

"Get it?" asks Aspen again.

"We all get it, *beta*," murmurs PapaDum, lifting pieces
of sizzling meat with the long tongs. (He upcycled the bar-
becue out of a wheelbarrow they found one Garbage Night.
It's really handy for wheeling the ashes to the compost.)

"Piece of chicken, Dad?" asks PopCorn. "Sausage?
Halloumi kebab? That's cheese."

The old man shakes his head.

"FYI, I caught the pike in the lake this morning,"
says Wood.

The fish sits frowning on a platter, as if it's offended
that nobody wants to eat it.

Grumps drinks from his glass, then chokes. "What
kind of grapefruit do you call this?"

"Watermelon," says Catalpa, "freshly squeezed, from
the community garden MaxiMum runs."

"Helps run," MaxiMum corrects her.

The old man nudges his glass away from him.

Sumac meets Catalpa's eyes, and they share a grimace. He doesn't have to drink it, but it's rude to shove it away as if it's toxic slime.

The grilled cubes of halloumi are scorching hot, but Sumac loves their saltiness. Brian pants and chews frantically.

"*Pelinti*," cries Sic.

"What does that mean?" asks Sumac, nibbling chicken off the bone. Sic's like Humpty Dumpty in *Through the Looking-Glass*: He enjoys taking words out for exercise.

"Don't encourage him," Catalpa tells her.

"Since you ask," says Sic, "*pelinti* is a Ghanaian word for shoving food around with your tongue while your mouth is open, to avoid getting scalded."

Sic is such a clever-clogs, Sumac thinks, he makes her seem nearly normal.

"I've got pics of the *Sligo*," he says in their grandfather's direction. "I need to edit them down from like five hundred —"

"*After* dinner," several parents chime, so Sic reluctantly puts his phone away.

Grumps has accepted a steak and a few vegetables.

"Any treasure on board the *Sligo*?" asks Wood glumly.

"Just limestone for road building," says PapaDum. "She sank in a storm in the last months of World War I."

"Were you in that one, Grammy?" Aspen cries suddenly.

Everyone stares at her. *Grammy?*

"Tell us about life in the olden days, do!"

Freak, Wood mouths at Aspen . . . who rolls up her tongue and pulls down her lower eyelids to show him the red bits.

Sumac figures it out: That was Aspen's quoting tone. They must be lines from the video she watched about dementia. Aspen usually seems to be goofing off instead of paying attention, but stuff sticks in her memory like chewing gum on her shoes. "Technically he'd need to be about a hundred and twenty to have been in World War I," Sumac whispers to her.

"Technically you sound more like fifty than nine, you know that?" Wood tells her.

"Let's keep it civil, and eat up," says MaxiMum. "How were your guide dogs this morning, Catalpa?"

"*So* smart. Like, if you give them the command to go forward but they see danger, they have to refuse, because their job is to know what's best for their human."

"Huh," says CardaMom. "Sounds like parenthood."

The grandfather doesn't seem to find that funny. He lets out an awful Gollumy cough. He's piling all the pieces of grilled eggplant way over on one side of his plate, Sumac notices, as if they're dirty.

Oak's wedged an entire corncob into his mouth. "You've bitten off more than you can chew, baby," CardaMom tells him, tugging it out.

"Ghah," says Oak.

"May I get down?" Aspen asks from the lawn.

"You appear to be down already," says PapaDum.

"You've only had, what, half a drumstick?" says CardaMom. "You're going to waste away."

Sometimes, looking at Aspen's boniness and CardaMom's thick middle, it's nearly impossible to believe that one of them came out of the other's body.

"And an asparagus spear and a half a *huge* slice of zucchini," calls Aspen, already halfway down the Wild, stroking Topaz.

The dessert is something called cranachan. "You like oatmeal and raspberries and cream," PapaDum reminds Brian.

"Not *musheded*," she says disgustedly. She slides off the bench and heads back to the big cardboard box that their last computer came in, which she's painting red for some reason.

"And here's the adult version," says PopCorn, pushing a full bowl toward his father. "D'you remember Mum used to add as much Scotch as cream?"

No comment. But Grumps does eat it, at least.

It's getting dark now: Fireflies blink their tiny lamps in the bushes. Farther down the Wild, Aspen and Brian are battling with lightsabers.

Sic burps as he pushes away his empty bowl. "Excuse me, peeps. *Shemomedjamo!*"

This time, Sumac stops herself from asking what that means. She spoons up her last smear of pink cream instead.

"I can tell by the general stunned silence that you're all wondering —"

"Whether you'll ever shut up, know-it-all," says Catalpa.

"Ah, you flatter me, sis. I wouldn't say I know it *all,*" says Sic, "just most things. It's been posited that not since 1800 has it been possible for one person to have a grasp on the sum total of human knowledge. No, I prefer to call myself simply a prodigy, a genius, if you will, a —"

Wood reaches across the table with two hands and presses his brother's mouth shut so hard that Sic's eyes bulge.

Grumps is squinting at the two of them, the way a sniper would look through the sights of his rifle.

All this squabbling and messing around was fun till the old man came, Sumac thinks. Now it's embarrassing, because he's watching and judging. And what gives him the right? Grumps has got butter all down his shirt, she notices, and he's picking something out of his teeth with one ridged

120

nail. How come the Lotterys were supposed to improve their table manners for this guy?

Sumac is suddenly so miserable, the only way she can think to cheer herself up is to go lie on her bed with a big stack of books. . . .

But her bed isn't her bed anymore, Sumac remembers as she carries her plate into the Mess, and her room isn't her room. She smacks down the plate so hard, she's afraid she's cracked it.

She toils up the three flights of stairs. Everything's off in the room Sumac still thinks of as Spare Oom: how the light slants in, the heavy slope of the ceiling (like a box some giant's crushed with his foot), the way the bed's facing — and the mattress is way too hard. The walls are a boring shade of nothing. Sumac picked these pale blue curtains — out of PopCorn's trunk of fabrics from all over the world — because they were the nearest thing to her sky mural, but now she hates them. This summer, nothing's the way it was or the way it should be.

✷

It's just nine of them going to the beach on Saturday, because Catalpa's busy in her mysterious teenage way, and PapaDum's taken Grumps to the dentist.

"Aspen," says MaxiMum, stepping out the front door into the glare of the sun, "I'm intrigued that you've chosen your roller shoes for cycling to the beach."

"Don't have any others."

MaxiMum allows herself a single roll of the eyes. "You have many others."

"Yeah, but where?"

"Can we go already?" asks Wood, sinking a basketball in one graceful arc across the Hoopla.

"Have you tried the Loseded and Finded?" Sumac asks Aspen. The gigantic tub down in the Mud Room used to be called the Lost and Found, but Brian's version of the name is the one that's stuck.

"I keep forgetting to," admits Aspen.

"Run!" CardaMom urges her.

"Come *on*, people, let's get moving," says Wood. "Sumac!"

He hurls the ball so hard, she catches it against her ribs and it knocks the breath out of her. She weighs up whether to complain or play. She frowns at the hoop and aims at it. . . .

But the ball bounces off the stonework, way too high, and shoots past the Zhaos' bungalow just as their brown bulgy car is backing out.

Mrs. Zhao blares the horn as if Sumac's thrown a hand grenade under her wheels.

"Sorry," shouts Sumac, not knowing whether she should race to retrieve the ball, or whether that means the woman will run her down. She wipes her forehead and smiles ditheringly.

"Don't take it personally, that hag doesn't like anyone," says Wood as the car — which Brian calls the Poop Cube — disappears down the street.

"Not even Mr. Zhao?" asks Sumac.

"Him least of all."

"Hard to be sure of that, because we've never heard Mr. Zhao speak any English, and other languages often sound angry if you don't know them," CardaMom points out.

"But remember that Christmas I went over with a plate of PapaDum's quadruple chocolate cookies, just out of the oven," says PopCorn, hurrying down the steps, "and Mrs. Zhao claimed they *didn't eat cookies?*" He starts fiddling with the combination lock of the bicycle cage. "Is it SWIFT? SWEAT? I thought a word would be easier to remember than numbers."

CardaMom grins, pushing him aside. "You know too many words. It's SPEED."

Brian comes down the steps one at a time, carrying a big plastic shovel and pail.

"Guess who gets to ride in the high seat today?" PopCorn reaches for her.

A shake of the fuzzy head as Brian backs out of range. "I ride my red bike."

"Yeah, but the thing of it is, *tsi't-ha*," says CardaMom, "we're cycling a long, long way along the boardwalk to the beach, and —"

"Ride red bike no training wheels!"

"Honeychild —"

Aspen pops back out of the house, holding up a sandal and a rubber boot. (Both lefties, Sumac notices).

"That's my boot," roars Wood.

"She's not going to wear your boot," MaxiMum tells him. "OK, Aspen, stay in your rollers, but pass me the gizmo to take the wheels out, at least."

Aspen's eyes go vague.

"Isn't the gizmo on the hook just inside the door, where it lives?" asks CardaMom.

"It definitely *was*," says Aspen.

CardaMom leans her head against MaxiMum's bony shoulder for a moment. "Marry me and take me away from all this," she groans.

MaxiMum strokes her hair. "Aspen will wear her rollers, and if the wheels get bunged up with sand, she'll have learned something useful."

It always takes so long for the Lotterys to leave the house, Sumac really should have asked for screen time so she could go back upstairs and do another twenty-minute strawberry on Mesopotamian customs.

But an hour later, as she stands up to her waist in Lake Ontario, reading *Tintin in Tibet*, she has to admit that this is a good place to be. A whole day stretching ahead without the new grandfather in it . . .

Back on shore, Sumac finds PopCorn trying to nap under a wonky tepee of sarongs stretched over driftwood, with the *New Yorker* magazine over his face. Oak keeps burying PopCorn's enormous feet in the sand and choking with laughter when the toes reappear. Brian won't wear her sun hat, so her head's all slippery with sunblock, except for patches where sand has stuck to the fuzz.

CardaMom press-gangs Sumac into some complicated ecological game in which Brian's playing the invasive zebra mussel, Wood's a rare bald eagle, and Sumac's the native sturgeon fish he's trying to catch. (Aspen was the sturgeon, but now she's way out in the lake, floating on her back.)

"What be Oak?" Brian wants to know.

"Ah . . ." Sumac considers her little brother in the sand. His crawling's getting much faster.

"The water," suggests CardaMom.

"You water, Oaky-doke. Wavy wavy!" Brian mimes it for him.

He waves his sandy fist. Wood strolls up to grab a banana.

"Oh, I have a joke," says Sumac, remembering.

Wood makes a sound of pain.

"Maybe it's a bit too hot for jokes," murmurs CardaMom.

"No, it has to be now because it's to do with bald eagles," says Sumac. "What's the only bird that needs to wear a wig?"

"Threw it away again," Wood tells her, shaking his head in disgust. "If you hadn't said in advance about the bald eagle, that would almost have been funny."

Sumac scowls.

Bringing her book over to where PopCorn lies in the shadow of the driftwood tepee, she flops down beside him. From the sound of his breathing she can tell he's not actually asleep. Remembering the population of Faro, she finds a pencil in the swim bag and does long division in the margin of his fallen magazine. (She could use the calculator app on a parent's phone, but she needs the mental exercise.) "Did you know for every Faro neighbor your dad used to say hi to, in Toronto there's . . . seven thousand two hundred and eighty-nine people."

"Huh," says PopCorn. "When you put it that way —"

"No wonder he's a bit out of sorts. Good point, Sumac," calls CardaMom from behind a music score.

Was that her point?

CardaMom goes on, "Think of having to leave everything you know five thousand kilometers behind, with no warning. . . ."

That's even worse than having to move bedrooms, it occurs to Sumac. She's suddenly so sorry for Grumps she feels a bit sick.

"Who?" says Aspen, practicing headstands beside PopCorn.

"My dad," he says.

"How much longer's he staying?"

Sumac sighs. "Do you never listen?"

"It's not your sister's forte," PopCorn reminds her. "We're going to give it a few weeks and see how we all rub along," he tells Aspen.

"I've got other fortes," she says, a little breathless as she straightens one leg in the air, then the second. "At least forty fortes!" She drops sideways onto him.

PopCorn lets out a scream — which makes the couple near them stare — then pretends to die, so the girls have to do CPR and defibrillation on him (with stones for the electric paddles), which is always good for a laugh.

"We were thinking you could be your grandfather's guide," says MaxiMum, coming over with a flask of water.

It's Sumac she's looking at.

Sumac stares. A *guide*, like Catalpa's dogs? *We were thinking?* Which of the parents was dumb enough to suggest that? Isn't it enough that Sumac has to give up her room to the intruder, who's messing up the whole summer?

"Just for the first while," calls CardaMom. "Show him round, explain how we do things. . . ."

Sumac keeps her lips pressed together, because if she lets out even half of what she's thinking, CardaMom's brown eyes will fill with disappointment.

She sidles off up the beach, drawing a long line in the sand with her foot. She thinks of writing a message: *SOS!*

Sic's heading back to shore with his splashy front crawl. Sumac waits till he's walking through the foam. "So what do you make of him?"

Sic knows who she means. "Mm, a wee bit dour, in't he?" he says in his best Scottish.

"What's dour?"

"Sulky." Sic pulls down the sides of his smile. "But you have to remember, the venerable dude was born in the thirties. He's, like, as old as television, older than the ballpoint pen."

The ballpoint pen? That stuns Sumac.

"Let's give him a while to learn our foreign ways," suggests Sic. "He'll crack under my barrage of charm in the end, everybody does."

"What's a barrage of —"

"Like, bombardment. Onslaught. Nonstop charm attack."

"Not everybody cracks under your barrage of charm," Sumac points out. "Those three girls from Vancouver at Camp Jagged Falls —"

"They were just pretending," he assures her. "It was, like, a thing between us."

A can't-stand-Sic-Lottery thing, Sumac thinks.

She goes back to the blanket to collect Oak, because he usually cheers her up. "Big splashes, Oaky?" She lugs him to where Wood's skimming stones and sits him down right in the foam.

Wood's searching through his pile for the most triangular flat ones. (Sumac knows the theory, but she just can't throw, and the last thing she's going to do is ask her brother for a lesson.) He skims one: It skips once, twice, then drops.

"What's your record?" she asks.

"Still eight." He throws one that lands with a big plop, and Oak laughs and does one of those claps where his hands miss and his plumpy arms smack instead. "When I'm eighteen, I might move over to the Islands," Wood says, nodding at the green shore across the water.

The thought of him — of any of her siblings — leaving home startles Sumac.

"They used to be a peninsula sticking out of Toronto," he adds.

"When, in caveman times?"

"No, right up till 1858," says Wood. He points west, to where the beach ends abruptly: "One night the Islands broke off in a storm."

She tries to picture it. The waves rising and crashing and the ground disappearing, so when you woke up the next morning, you were cut off from land. . . .

She picks Oak up, but he wails, so she dips his fat legs into the water again. "Belugas can dive down to seven hundred meters," she tells Wood.

"Oh yeah?"

"They live in unstable pods. That means if you're not enjoying the pod you're with, you can swim off and join another anytime."

"We've all had days like that," says Wood grimly.

Brian runs down to the water's edge now, with PopCorn and Aspen chasing behind because she's insisting on trying to float on her back without her *poopy peefdy*. (That's what she calls her PFD, for personal flotation device.)

They all stand there while Brian thrusts her tummy up so hard that lake water washes over her face and makes her splutter and stand again. And repeat. "How much of seconds?" she demands.

"One," says Sumac, rounding up a little.

Wood flicks a stone, dangerously close to his little sister.

"How much now?" Brian stands up, coughing out water.

"Ah . . . one and a half seconds," says PopCorn. "Tummy high, like a cake rising!"

"How much?" splutters Brian the next time, clawing something green off her cheek.

"I — sorry, sprog," he says, "I wasn't counting that time."

"Count! Watch me, Oaky." She throws herself backward.

Sumac's arms are getting tired, so she gives Oak one more ducking to his grubby neck, then passes him to PopCorn, who's scratching a sunburned bit of his neck tattoo.

"You not counting!" Brian roars at them, water in her eyes that could be lake or tears. "I was floating for hours and hours and you —"

"Sorry," they all tell her.

She heaves backward into the water, stiff with outrage.

"One!" Three voices, with enthusiasm. "Two —"

But Brian's sunk already. She rears up. "How much that time?"

"One and three-quarter seconds," says Sumac. Her little sister is pretty brave, but she's not going to be able to swim for years yet.

"Is your dad going to stay till his dimension's better?" Aspen asks suddenly.

PopCorn doesn't correct her this time. "If that does definitely turn out to be what he's got, it doesn't really . . . get better."

Sumac pictures a cheese, with holes getting bigger.

"You should cancel him," says Aspen.

He squints at her. "Is that some kind of threat? I should rub him out, like the Mafia would?"

"No! Use your canceling."

He whoops with laughter.

"*Counseling*'s what he used to work at, you twit," calls Wood. "Talking about feely-weelings."

"*Canceling* means making something stop," Sumac explains to Aspen.

"Same difference," says her sister with a shrug. "Make him talk about his feelings till he stops leaving things in the deep fryer."

Sumac almost chokes, pointing at Brian. Eyes shut against the sunlight, their four-year-old bobs on the surface of the water: a pale, bald starfish.

Brian blinks up at them. "How much of seconds?"

Nobody speaks.

"You all talking again," she growls, exploding out of the water.

"No, you floated so long we lost count!" The words burst out of Sumac.

"Yeah," says Aspen, "we seriously ran out of numbers."

Brian grins like a pike.

"She did it," PopCorn bawls back to CardaMom on the sand. "She can float!" He lifts Oak into the air and plays him like a saxophone.

"A million of seconds?" Brian wants to know.

"Infinity," says Aspen.

Technically, those are both exaggerations, but for once Sumac buttons her lip.

✷

After dinner, she's waiting in the Hall of Mirrors, outside the room that for nine and a bit years used to be hers. Standing ready, like a guide dog — even though she never exactly said yes to MaxiMum; she just didn't pluck up the courage to say no.

When the dogs are helping someone, Catalpa says, they have to wear a stiff harness that says *DO NOT PET ME I AM WORKING*.

Somebody's added Iain to the bottom of the Where Board, Sumac notices. Opposite his name, in the blank space for where he is, she's tempted to write *In the Wrong Place* or *Where He's Not Wanted*.

Instead, she stares at the latest inspiring quote printed —
in CardaMom's lipstick, it looks like — on an old gilt-framed
mirror.

No man is an island.
— John Donne

Is that *man*, as in, everyone, like in old books? Sumac
thinks about the peninsula that woke up one morning to
find it was an island. She wishes her no-longer-dormant
grandfather was living on a island somewhere far away.

"Sumac?" says MaxiMum, stepping out and beckoning her.

She makes a grim face; she can't help it.

MaxiMum surprises her by pulling a worse one, with
crossed eyes and a mad-rabbit overbite, which almost makes
Sumac laugh out loud.

She steps past MaxiMum, over the threshold. "Hi," she
says, and clears her throat.

Creepy: It's not Sumac's bedroom anymore, but Grumps
hasn't made it into his either. There's a faintly sour smell
that she doesn't think is cigarettes. He still hasn't unpacked,
just opened one suitcase full of crumpled shirts and pants.
The painted blue sky looks sort of shabby now, and there's a

cracked bit on one of the clouds that Sumac never noticed. "What would you like to know about us?" she asks.

A shrug as Grumps stares out the window at the side of the Zhaos' bungalow.

MaxiMum's slipped away already.

"Will I quiz you on our names, maybe?"

"Will you what?"

"Ask you what we're called, like in a quiz."

"I'm all right."

Does that mean he knows all the names, or that he couldn't care less what his grandchildren are called?

A red cube trots by the window: That's Brian in her fire truck going around the side of the house. She put the painted box on as soon as she finished it this afternoon and won't take it off, so the strings are making marks on her shoulders. Sumac helped her poke holes for the paper-plate wheels, but Brian attached them to the sides of the box with the paper fasteners herself and covered the headlights (two more paper plates) with foil to make them shiny. Brian's pretty good at making things, when she's not in a rage. The fire truck was only a two-and-a-half-rage project, which is not bad. For Brian's fourth birthday, Gram (their grandmother from Jamaica, MaxiMum's mom) gave her a Make Your Own Pirate Treasure Chest kit, even though it said *8+* right on the box, and that turned out to be a seven-rager.

Sumac takes a step toward the door. "If you don't have any questions . . ."

"Which of ye keeps forgetting to flush the toilet?"

She blinks. "If it's brown?"

Grumps stares at her as if she's said something filthy.

She feels herself blushing and looks at the bare boards, where her lovely soft rug used to lie. "Like the signs on the tanks say. *If it's brown, flush it down,*" she chants in a very small voice, "*but if it's yellow, let it mellow.*" An awful pause. "It saves about six liters every time."

The old man throws out his hand toward the south. "Ye live on a lake too big to see across!"

"Yeah, but . . ." Sumac wishes one of the teenagers or parents were here to explain it better. "See, if all the water on the planet was in a glass —" She looks around. "Do you have a glass of water?"

"Why would I?"

"To drink. In the night."

"Don't like water," says Grumps, "day or night."

Sumac is thrown by that. "OK, well, imagic — imagine," she corrects herself. "Ninety-seven percent of the water in the glass would be salty, right?"

"Why would you fill a glass with salty water?"

"It's a metaphor," she says. "And nearly all the rest, the last three percent of all the water in the world, is frozen or filthy. So there's only zero point one eight percent that's drinkable, and we have to share it with all the other living things."

"Just as well I never touch the stuff, then, isn't it?"

Was that a joke? Grumps is not smiling.

Sumac struggles to find a new subject. "Would you like . . . maybe a tour of all the bits of Camelottery you haven't seen yet?"

"Of what?"

"This house."

"Nae thank you." That didn't sound polite, even if it did include a thank you.

Upstairs in the Theater it sounds like Brian's watching *Frozen*, which Sumac only pretends to not like anymore. She wonders whether she's spent long enough in this bare, nasty-smelling room that she can leave without a parent asking why she isn't being a guide dog.

"What age were you when you landed up here?" Grumps asks suddenly.

She's startled by the question. "Ah, two hours."

"Aren't you one of those wee girlies from a Chinese orphanage?"

"No I'm not." But Sumac supposes he's trying to make

conversation, in his unpleasant way, so she goes on, "The moms and dads brought me straight from the hospital in a cab."

Sic always claims that he, at seven, had the casting vote on whether the Lotterys wanted a fifth baby. He says that because Number Four (Aspen) was barely walking, he only agreed to another little sister on the condition that this one would Revere and Obey Him at All Times. Sumac doesn't exactly revere Sic, but she does adore him.

"My birth mom's Filipina, by the way," she adds, just so the old man won't think she doesn't know, "and my birth dad's ancestors are from Germany."

His forehead crinkles up.

"My bios aren't a couple. And they didn't want to be anybody's mom or dad," she spells out.

"Why not?"

"Dunno. Did you want to be a dad?" Sumac asks, thinking of PopCorn-the-ugly-baby in the faded photos.

The wet old eyes blink at her. "Not particularly," Grumps says as if to himself, "but these things sort themselves out, I suppose."

"Nenita's in Ottawa but she travels all the time for work," says Sumac, trying to think of something else to say. "Jensen lives about twenty hours' drive away in Manitoba."

She doesn't mention that they're both accountants, because that sounds weird.

"Never heard the like," murmurs Grumps. "Do they come see you at all, these whatchamacallem, bio people?"

"Oh yeah," says Sumac. Though never at the same time. She thinks Nenita and Jensen's what-will-we-do-about-the-baby conversation probably happened over email.

Grumps has put just one thing on the desk that used to be hers: a calendar of *Wildflowers of Yukon*. The July page shows a little purple blossom. He's drawn diagonal slashes through the seventeenth, eighteenth, nineteenth, and twentieth. Ah, it's the days he's been in Toronto, Sumac realizes.

Day one of his stay, CardaMom said, but a *stay* is what you have in a hotel, until you go home. If you're really going to stay somewhere *for the moment, for the present*, it's not called a stay. Prisoners *do time*. That's what the lines through the dates are like: the scratches a prisoner makes on a cell wall.

The old man's eyes have followed Sumac's

to the calendar. "The whole crew of ye'll be on your holliers for months, I suppose."

"On our what?"

"School holidays."

"Oh, we don't go to school," says Sumac.

"What, never?" he asks with a kind of horror. "Ye stay at home all the time?"

Sumac shakes her head. "We learn by doing, mostly. Like, tomorrow's outing, it's to Buskerfest." PopCorn's challenged Sumac to interview a performer about how they acquired their skills and edit it into a five-minute video. She knows exactly who she's going to ask too: an amazing woman she saw last year who can spin seven burning hoops around her arms and legs at the same time. "You know, buskers? People who play music and stuff, and pass a hat around?"

"Beggars, they were called in my day."

Sumac tries something else. "PapaDum said maybe you'd like to join us for a stroll this evening, to see the neighborhood?"

"I was down the shops already this morning. It all smells a bit Third World."

"That's only because it's so hot and they were collecting the garbage," says Sumac, on the brink of losing her temper.

Grumps's eyes are shut now, and he's rubbing his papery forehead as if it hurts.

"Are you tired? Do you need to go to bed early? CardaMom said you might nap in the afternoons, like Oak."

The eyes crack open again, blue as ice. "Like what?"

"Oak, our baby."

"Young lady, I've never had a nap in my born days."

Sumac makes a final effort. Stick to the past, not the present. "It was World War II you were alive in, wasn't it? What was it like?"

"None of your beeswax, nosey parker."

Sumac doesn't have to stand here and take this abuse, so she walks out without another word.

CHAPTER 7

COMPOS MENTIS

On Saturday morning, Sumac finds MaxiMum way at the back of the Wild, cross-legged, sitting. (That's what Buddhists call *meditating*, like skateboarders just say *skating*.) Topaz is pressed against one of her knees.

"Need something, Sumac?" asks MaxiMum, eyes shut, when Sumac's still about three meters away.

"No, sorry," she whispers, backing away.

"It's OK, I'm done," says MaxiMum, standing up in one fluid twist and stretching her endlessly long arms above her head. Topaz stalks away, offended.

"Two questions," says Sumac, improvising so it won't seem as if she interrupted the meditation for nothing.

MaxiMum drops into a squat, then stands and bends backward so her voice comes out upside down. "First question?"

"How come you can see us with your eyes shut?"

She laughs. "You each breathe differently. Aspen's the easiest because there are always sound effects as well." MaxiMum straightens up and jiggles on the spot as an illustration.

"Second question," says Sumac, very quietly. "You didn't vote yes, did you?"

MaxiMum doesn't pretend she doesn't know what Sumac means. Instead, she shrugs. "Four parents . . . I can't expect to get my own way more than seventy-five percent of the time."

Sumac frowns. "That's bad math."

MaxiMum winks, holding one foot behind her now, arching like the medieval bow Wood's been working on all summer.

"And anyway, I bet PapaDum voted no too, which means

it must have been fifty-fifty," says Sumac. What she's working her way around to is, now they've seen what the old man is like to live with, can they have a proper Fleeting about him, this time with all the Lotterys voting on whether he stays or goes? "So what I was wondering is, what if —"

"Sumac." MaxiMum puts a hand up to stop her. "The four of us don't exactly vote on things. We decide together the best we can."

Yeah, you decide by leaving us kids out.

"You're not a big fan of change, are you?"

"I am sometimes," Sumac protests. She tries to think of an example. "Adopting Brian and Oak, that was totally my idea." (She wanted to be a big sister, for once, instead of always the little one.)

"I'd forgotten," says MaxiMum, grinning. "And that worked out, didn't it?"

But that was different, because the Lotterys all had a pretty good idea it would be fun to have more kids. Whereas an old man who never opens his mouth except to say something grouchy . . .

"I'm going to have my shower now," says MaxiMum.

Sumac sighs. "I should pack my bag for Buskerfest."

"Ah, change of plan: We're going to Pedestrian Saturday at Kensington Market instead," says MaxiMum. "We thought, a bit less crowded, and Iain might like the leather place, or the canning store. Plus, there's tango dancing with a live orchestra."

Sumac presses her teeth together hard. Is she the most bad-tempered, unwelcoming Lottery? Or is she the miner's canary — the first to notice how this old man's wrecking everything?

✱

The day was indeed a total washout. Grumps kept complaining about the smell of incense and saying the whole market was *wall-to-wall hippy tat*. At the I Scream, their favorite gelateria, he wouldn't even try a half scoop of anything because there were no *ordinary flavors*. Sumac wished he'd stayed home on his own, but Sic told her that wouldn't be safe, because he might burn Camelottery down too. Sumac's still not sure whether that was a joke.

Then, on Sunday, the Lotterys were going to try out a Bahá'í meeting, but instead they ended up taking Grumps to a really boring Presbyterian church because he'd find it familiar, and afterward he claimed he didn't recognize any of the hymns anyway. So it seems to Sumac that when they change all their plans for this old man, it doesn't make anybody happy.

He drifts around Camelottery like a headless ghost. Whenever he comes into a room, one of the Lotterys jumps up to help him find what he's looking for, but by then he's already muttered something and gone out again. Sumac has made diagrams of each floor with enormous labels, in thirty-six-point font, and stuck them up on the landings, but it doesn't seem to make any difference.

Now it's Monday morning and CardaMom's opening a week's worth of mail — standing up at the counter, because she says sitting makes her sluggish. One card has silver feathers embossed on it, like that earring that CardaMom's only got one of now, since Aspen played Treasure Hunt with the other. It says in old-fashioned script that *Mary Johnson* (that's CardaMom) *plus one* are invited as special guests to a Gala Gathering of Indigenous Women Leading Change.

"Why are you a Woman Leading Change?" asks Sumac.

CardaMom grins. "I've just sat on some committees and boards and donated a bunch of our lottery winnings."

Funny thing, the parents are pretty mean when it comes to spending, but they're always giving it away. "Who's the *plus one*?" asks Sumac.

"Oh, that means a partner or loved one."

"So, MaxiMum."

"Don't you forget it," says MaxiMum, muffled, as she stands sorting tubs in the freezer.

CardaMom blows a kiss at her. "But really you're all my loved ones."

"Your Loved Many," suggests Sumac.

"Well put," says CardaMom. "I'll RSVP to say I'm bringing my *plus ten*, if they can rustle up enough chairs."

Sumac giggles at the image of that.

She stops as Grumps comes in. She watches his eighty-two-year-old legs crossing the Mess. They work just fine, so actually he could have stayed in Spare Oom, and Sumac could have kept her beloved bedroom. . . .

Aspen runs in brandishing her cat's cradle string. "What do you all want to see me do, Lizard Twist or Cheating the Hangman?"

"How about showing us Eat French Toast, and then Put Plate in Dishwasher?" suggests PapaDum, setting a teapot down between Grumps and PopCorn.

Aspen's face brightens. "I'll do Two Diamonds but call it Two Plates. Prepare to be amazed, because I can do it in six seconds with my eyes shut!"

As her fingers start working, a low moan emerges from PopCorn and his knee bounces.

MaxiMum pats him on the shoulder. "Let's remember that cat's cradle strengthens concentration, memory, and hand-eye coordination."

"Done," squeals Aspen, holding up the shape.

"It's, let's see, nonelectronic," adds CardaMom. "An indigenous game that kids have invented everywhere from the Arctic to the equator . . ."

"Yeah, and one of these days I'm going to strangle her with that string," mutters PopCorn.

"Hate speech and death threats, you goin' to jail," crows Aspen.

Grumps slurps his tea.

"Catalpa, Empress of the Night?" asks PopCorn.

Wandering in like a sleepwalker, Catalpa yawns in his direction.

"What's your goal, your passion, your quest for today?"

"Waking up." Lush eyelashes resting on her cheeks.

"How's your graphic design course coming along?" asks PapaDum.

"Coming along," she murmurs, taking a piece of French toast and nibbling it.

Thunk, thunk: Sic bounds into the Mess on his pogo stick.

"Get *off* that thing," orders Catalpa, covering her ears.

He jumps down. "Up late cyberjamming with Game of Groans, were we?"

"Game of *Tones!*"

Sniggers around the table.

"I never sleep, hardly," Aspen boasts. "I always get up in the night and play and try not to wake people."

Grumps snorts.

"Does she disturb you, Iain?" asks CardaMom.

No answer.

"At least I don't flush the toilet," says Aspen, triumphant.

Nobody dares smile.

"Anyway. OK if I go rehearse at someone's place this afternoon?" asks Catalpa.

"A real-world experience," marvels PopCorn. "Whose house?"

"Probably Quinn's."

"Leave us her parents' number."

"So hey, speaking of real-world activities," says Sic, "would you guys be cool with covering the application fee for my learner's license?"

"Are you still at this?" asks PapaDum, shaking his head in wonder.

"Do you need a license to drive . . . your parents mad?" Aspen asks, bouncing up and down on her ball. "Get it? Get it?"

"We get it," MaxiMum assures her.

Aspen's jokes aren't always so hilarious either, Sumac thinks.

Grumps doesn't seem to hear any of this. But he's not deaf; Sumac is pretty sure of that now. It's as if the Lotterys are seagulls and he's just shutting his ears to their yakking and yawping.

"This is an educational qualification we're talking about, Moms 'n' Pops," says Sic, hand on heart.

"So is a hot air balloon pilot's license," MaxiMum tells him, "but not one you're in immediate need of, given that we don't own a hot air balloon."

"That's defeatist thinking."

CardaMom hoots with laughter and leans across the table to kiss Sic on the nose, knocking over a not-quite-empty jug of milk with her chest.

"Argh." Sumac lifts up her glass so it doesn't get wet.

"Uh-oh," Oak sings out.

"This house!" That's Catalpa.

"Sorry," cries CardaMom, running for a cloth.

"So was that kiss a yes?" Sic wants to know.

"No, treasure," says CardaMom, "it was a kiss."

"What about chipping in, say, seventy percent, to encourage me," says Sic, "because I'm growing my skills instead of lying around reading sword-and-sorcery and scratching my bug bites all summer?"

Catalpa reaches out to thump him, but he blocks her fist with his plate.

"You need encouragement like a giraffe needs a longer neck," she tells him.

Aspen mimes the giraffe, making everyone laugh. Well, everyone except Grumps.

"C'mon, work with me, people," begs Sic. "Fifty percent?"

"Maybe thirty?" suggests PopCorn, looking between the other parents.

"Forty percent, we have a deal!" Sic punches the air and nobody contradicts him.

"Were you out early this morning?" PapaDum asks Wood, who's just come in.

"Sunrise," he says with a nod. "Saw a rabbit, a red cardinal, two snakes — probably eastern garters, but they were pretty small so they could have been Butler's garters, except they slid off too fast for me to count the scale rows."

"Do you think they were mother and baby?" Sumac asks.

Wood shrugs. "They looked about the same size, but I don't know how long snakes take to grow up."

Aspen rolls back on her ball so far that she nearly falls on her butt. "Are they monotonous?"

"Not to me," snaps Wood. "Now cat's freakin' cradle, that's what I'd call monotonous."

"What *monotonous*?" asks Brian.

"Boring," Sumac tells her.

Aspen shakes her head, brown hair falling in her eyes. "Monotonous like *pears*."

That puzzles everyone.

"Juicy pears?" asks Brian.

"No! Married."

"She means do snakes live in *pairs*, couples," says Sumac after a second.

"*Monogamous!* Our code breaker," says PopCorn, squeezing Sumac's neck.

"Great question, Aspen, and I'm stumped," says MaxiMum. "Family life of snakes, anyone?"

"I doubt they're monogamous," says Catalpa. "Not with their slithery, sneaky reputation."

Wood rolls his eyes. "That's just squeamish humans making up lies about them. Bees kill way more people in Ontario than snakes do."

"Only in self-defense," says Sumac hotly. "You owe every third bite of that to a bee —" and she pokes Wood's French toast.

"Hands off my food!" Wood slaps her fingers away.

"Let's keep it civil," says MaxiMum.

"Snakeses be married?" asks Brian.

"Yes, that was our original question, wasn't it? I challenge Wood to find out."

"Wolves." The word erupts from Grumps.

"What's that, Iain?" asks CardaMom with a smile. "What about wolves?"

"One male, one female, paired for life. It's nature's way."

Sumac checks the parents' faces, which have all gone stony. "Oh, Dad, I think you'll find nature's got lots of different ways," says PopCorn.

Grumps makes a humph sound. "One male," he says again, "one female."

The silence feels like static to Sumac, as if any second now, she'll get an electric shock. Sic is not smiling, for once. Catalpa's sucking her lips and Wood's doing his tough-guy stare. Aspen's the only one who's oblivious, eyes almost shut as she makes a Jacob's Ladder with her string.

"Uh-oh!" says Oak.

PapaDum examines a fresh scratch on Wood's cheekbone. "You should put antibiotic cream on that."

"Yeah, yeah." Which they all know means he won't.

"May I be excused?" asks Aspen, jumping up.

"Did you eat your French toast?" CardaMom asks.

The plate Aspen's holding high in the air like a waiter is empty. "I suspect someone else did," says MaxiMum.

"Increased nutritional needs of puberty," says Wood, thumping his chest like a gorilla.

"OK, but let's have another go at your twelve times tables this morning," MaxiMum says to Aspen . . . who lets out a groan as if she's been stabbed.

"Keep at it," PapaDum tells her. *"No use climbing halfway up a coconut tree."*

"Is that one of your wise Indian proverbs?" asks Sumac.

"You know me well," says PapaDum in his father's accent, waggling his head.

When you're halfway up a coconut tree, you've done half the work but you don't have half the coconut yet. So yeah, Sumac supposes, it would be a waste to slither down again. . . .

"Got to rush." PopCorn stands up too. "I'm running Parent Break around the corner in twenty minutes." (That means parents get two hours off while PopCorn's doing his charming Pied Piper thing at the kids' center, but he jokes that it's called that because it's for parents who are about to break.) "Who wants to teach tinies how to make sparkle lanterns?"

None of the other Lotterys seem to be in the mood for volunteering today.

"I'm working toward breaking the world record for most jumps," says Sic, brandishing his pogo stick, "which, as you'll all recall, is two hundred and six thousand, eight hundred and sixty-four, in twenty hours, thirteen minutes."

Sumac seizes the moment. "I know a funny joke about jumping."

"Dude, it kills it when you start like that," says Wood. "Makes us all tense."

"Yeah," Sic tells her, "why don't you just slide it into conversation, and if by some miracle we laugh, then hey, score!"

Sumac scowls. "Do you want to hear my joke or not?"

"Is that a rhetorical question?" groans Catalpa.

"Full marks for persistence, anyway," says PapaDum.

"Here goes." Sumac clears her throat. "What dog can jump higher than a building?"

"Hm," CardaMom starts, "what dog —"

"Any dog," says Aspen in a bored robot voice, "because buildings can't jump."

"I could tell jokes just fine if you'd stop stealing my punch lines," roars Sumac.

Sic gives her a sympathetic grin before heading out.

"Don't forget your helmet," MaxiMum calls.

He shakes his head. "Forecast says the temperature's due to spike today, especially with the humidity, and my head's going to melt if I squish my 'fro into a helmet. Sixteen's old enough to make a reasoned decision not to look like a dork."

"The stuff you do with your goofy friends," says Wood, "unicycling, parkour, fountaineering — you realize none of them are actual sports?"

"Yeah," says Catalpa, "they're just attention seeking. You guys look like such dorks, with or without helmets, none of you will ever have a girlfriend."

"Right," says Sic, "whereas spending your summer scooping doggy doo makes you irresistible!"

CardaMom stacks plates in the dishwasher. "If growing up in this house hasn't taught you all not to care whether you look cool or not, then I'm going to give up and send you all to school."

"Ha ha ha," says Sic, doing a ghost train sound effect. "The same hollow threat you've been making for sixteen years."

They're all just chattering away as usual, thinks Sumac, looking at her grandfather, who's got his head down over his tea. As if Grumps is an accident in the highway, and the safest thing is to drive on by.

✱

Wednesday's Garbage Night, and they only get home when the sun's going down, with a good haul in Oak's bike chariot: a mannequin's hand and three polystyrene heads that could be great for making puppets, some only slightly scratched frames, lots of floppy roses to dry into petal confetti, a VHS player and a smoke alarm and a coffeemaker to take apart and study, two feather boas, and a fancy birdcage

Sharp-Eye Sumac spotted, which might be a hundred years old. "Though really the very best," she tells CardaMom on the stairs, "was when we saw a skunk with five babies coming up the alley, waving their tails."

"Fantastic," says CardaMom, in a whisper because Oak (in his sleep sack) is conked out on her, his hair all slick with sweat.

Sumac goes up on tiptoes to kiss her brother's ear — the left, more-sticky-out one that's always slightly creased.

"MaxiMum and I are going in the Hot Tub once I've put this fellow down," whispers CardaMom. "Could you knock on your grandfather's door and check he's taken his evening pills?"

Why me? is what Sumac wants to ask, but she knows the answer: She's the guide dog. Which was a huge ask, and they shouldn't have asked it in the first place, and she shouldn't have failed-to-say-no except that she didn't want her parents to stop thinking of her as such a *mature, helpful, rational being.*

"Here, Sumac," says MaxiMum, coming out of the moms' room with a tube. "I picked up more of his eyebrow cream."

So Sumac goes downstairs and makes herself tap on the door. It still has a tiny hole from the nail that held up the *Sumac's Room* sign. But the kids have started to call it the Grumpery (though there's no sign saying so, obviously).

A grunt from the other side. Sumac can't tell if it means come in or go away. She taps again. Is that tobacco she's smelling?

The door swoops open.

"Ah, hi. CardaMom wanted to remind you to take your medicine."

Grumps jerks his head a little. Does that mean he's already taken it and doesn't need reminding, or he has no intention of taking it? He's got a cigarette half-hidden behind him.

"Did you forget?" asks Sumac, pointing.

He looks at the cigarette as if it's somebody else's.

She scrunches up her nose. "Remember you have to go outside for that?"

"I didn't forget anything, missy," says Grumps. "I just

didn't think it was anybody's business what I do in my own room."

Sumac chews her lip. "Smoking kills."

"Who cares? I'm eighty-two," he says. But he steps back and stubs the cigarette out on a saucer.

Doesn't he realize he's probably giving all the Lotterys cancer, especially Oak, because he's closest to the ground, where the smoke hangs? Sumac takes a tiny step into the room that's so nasty now. "And here's more of the special cream to help your eyebrows grow back faster."

He rolls his eyes. "What call have I for eyebrows, at this point?"

Sumac is thrown by the question. Why does anyone need eyebrows? Are they to stop sweat running into our eyes? Or rain?

He takes the tube out of her hand anyway. "What's all the clatter and banging at this time of the evening?"

She explains about Garbage Night.

But she must not have done a very good job of it, because the old man is goggling at her. "Ye grub around in folks' rubbish?"

"It's scavenging, like a treasure hunt," she says, "and it's, you know, kind to the planet, especially as we clean up with trash pickers and pooper scoopers as we go along. We're like the Wombles." Would he ever have read the Wombles books? "Little bears who reuse and recycle?"

He snorts. "Gadzillionaires — have ye no shame?"

Sumac is suddenly very tired. There's that smell again, sort of stale and sweetish: She thinks it's him. "Why haven't you put anything up except your flower calendar?" He's drawn a line through seven of the days now.

"Won't be here much longer, will I?" says Grumps.

"Won't you?" That sounded way too eager. "Oh," Sumac tries again, in an almost regretful voice. What could he mean? Her eyes lodge on the purple flower of the calendar again. "What's the circle?" she asks, pointing to the thirty-first of July.

"D-day. D for Departure," says Grumps with satisfaction.

Her pulse starts to go bang-bang. That's a week from today. "Where are you departuring — departing to?"

"My own wee house in Faro, of course. *A couple of weeks, on a trial basis*, they said, *and we'll see*." The words are pouring out now, and Grumps's lip is spotty with spit. "When the fortnight's up, they'll have to admit that it's all been a botch and a bungle, because I'm fighting fit. *Mens sana in corpore sano*."

"Is that Spanish?" Sumac wonders.

"Do you not have a word of Latin?"

"I know some Sumerian," she says in a small voice.

Grumps thumps his chest with a hollow sound, then knocks on his head. *"A healthy mind in a healthy body* is what it means. Maybe not as sharp as I used to be in this department" — tapping his head again — "but that's par for the course. Getting older's not a disease! I've gone along with all this testing nonsense, let the whitecoats poke and prod and nag me, just to set Reginald's mind at rest that there's nothing serious the matter. I'm as *compos mentis* as he is — it's not me who believes in star signs and auras!"

It's the most Sumac's ever heard this old man say. Grumps sounds almost happy, for the first time. "You say you're compost —"

"More Latin: *compos mentis.* Look it up, as your colored mum's always saying."

Sumac steps out and shuts the door behind her, quite loudly: nearly a slam. He deserves it for calling MaxiMum *colored* in that sneery tone.

She marches upstairs to the treadmill desk and fingers through the big dictionary. *Compos mentis.* It sounds like minty compost. Found it: *Of sound or composed mind.*

Oh. So Grumps doesn't believe he's losing his marbles at all, or only a normal amount for eighty-two. Could it just possibly be like that time the doctor was worried

MaxiMum might have a kidney stone, but then she got the all clear?

It's true, PopCorn did say something about *a couple of weeks.* If all the rest of it is true — if it turns out it's all been a mistake about the dementia — then Grumps can go home, and everything at Camelottery can go back to normal! (Of course, he'd scoff at the idea that anything here is normal. How things used to be, then.)

Sumac jumps up and down on the treadmill. *Egg salad,* as Brian would say!

CHAPTER 8

FRIEND OR FOE

The Lotterys can't go to the Powwow this year (because *let's keep things simple*, which is code for having to look after Grumps). That means it'll be who knows how long before they see Baba — one of their real, nice grandfathers. When she hears this, Sumac so nearly blurts out, "But if his test results come back and he's *compos mentis* enough, he'll be flying home to Faro before the weekend." She manages to keep her mouth zipped, not wanting to count chickens before they hatch; if she says it out loud, it might not happen.

The old man spends most of his time sitting in his stark room, listening to classical music on the radio. Killing time like a prisoner in solitary confinement, Sumac supposes.

On Monday morning he says no to the beach, so MaxiMum wonders aloud if maybe he's not feeling up to the exertion in this heat. Grumps tells her he's in the pink of health, thank you very much, and no he doesn't need a taxi since he hasn't forgotten how to ride a bike yet, and he stomps off to get his towel. That's called reverse psychology; it's how the Lotterys trick Brian into changing her socks by saying maybe she's not able to do it all by herself.

PapaDum's staying home, because Oak's gone kaput in his stroller already, and also he's going to fix those sagging shelves in the Bookery and make seafood paella. (But really because he's a homebody who needs a Parent Break every now and then.) Whizzing along the cycle path at the back of the pack of Lotterys, Sumac stares at Grumps's pale hairy shanks going around and around on PapaDum's bike. She can't help wondering what the statistics are about people of eighty-two falling off bikes.

It's certainly true, what he said about his *healthy body*, so might it be true about his mind as well? Grumps doesn't exactly seem confused to Sumac; just cross, mostly. Could the parents have made a massive mistake?

But, hm, if somebody's got brain holes, one effect might be that he wouldn't realize about the holes. Also, the dads and moms are pretty smart if you add up all their different smarts. And the specialists and experts — wouldn't they have said if Grumps didn't have dementia after all? Then again, test results take ages. So Sumac will just have to cross her fingers and wish hard to be a perfectly sized family of eleven again.

On the beach, Sic, Catalpa, and Wood undo the bungee cords attaching their flat-packed kayak to Sic's bike and struggle to open it up. CardaMom holds a tiny PFD under one elbow and uses her hands to paste Brian's upper half with sunblock.

"What are you putting a life jacket on the child for?" asks Grumps, wobbling on one leg as he changes behind his towel. "In my day we just jumped in, or got pushed. *Learning by doing*," he quotes sarcastically. "Sink or swim." He lets out an awful gargling laugh.

Wide-eyed, Brian slides out of CardaMom's hands. "No poopy peefdy."

"C'mere, slippery fish."

"I swim no lessons like Napoleons."

"Mm, you back-floated really well the other day," says CardaMom, "but you still need your peefdy."

"I swim! I swim like Napoleons!"

Grumps walks off, eyes on the horizon — as if he hasn't just set Brian off like a firework, thinks Sumac in irritation. No goggles; he's wearing nothing but his raggedy old swim trunks. He stalks into the lake, then stoops to plunge in. He moves like a turtle, doing a strained-looking breaststroke with his nose held above the water.

"If Brian believes she can swim," says MaxiMum, raising her voice to be heard over the argument, "maybe she can."

Sumac can't believe MaxiMum's siding with their demented grandfather!

"She's four years old." CardaMom grabs Brian by the back of her shorts.

"Granted, but with physical skills — think of riding a bike," says MaxiMum. "There's an element of sheer confidence, which may be enough."

"Enough to let her drown like a kitten," roars CardaMom. Then, more calmly, "Brian, until you put your peefdy on, you're going to have to stay here with me instead of —"

"I swim, dumb fatty mother!"

CardaMom stares at her.

"Change of shift," murmurs MaxiMum, standing up and walking between them. "You go read *Pride and Prejudice* in the shade, darlin'."

"Are you seriously intending to let her go in without her PFD?"

"I'll be right there beside her, and if she sinks I'll pull her up."

"*If?*"

167

As the moms squabble on, Brian's racing toward the water.

Sumac pelts after her little sister. Grumps and his ludicrous olden-days ideas!

But MaxiMum is on Brian's tail already, so when she plunges in face-first, MaxiMum lifts her by her armpits. "Breathe."

"Let go," Brian coughs.

Sumac stubs her toe on an algae-slippery rock and hisses with pain.

"I *swim*," howls Brian.

"Big breath?" MaxiMum waits for it. Then puts Brian down.

She sinks under the water again.

"Pick her up," begs Sumac. "That's not swimming, that's drowning."

MaxiMum watches the little lashing fury. "It could be argued that swimming means drowning a bit, getting back to the surface, drowning a bit again. . . ."

"Pick her up!" Sumac claws her way toward her sister to save her —

But Brian's up again, under her own steam, splashing and gasping, doggy-paddling.

MaxiMum puts her hands up. "Didn't touch you."

"I swim," Brian pants.

"Apparently so." Though MaxiMum is hovering just inches away, Sumac notices.

"No more poopy peefdy *ever*." Then Brian swallows some lake water, and chokes, and coughs.

MaxiMum scoops her up.

"Sorry I screamed at you," says Sumac, her voice uneven. "I was just worried."

"You're an excellent worrier," MaxiMum tells her.

Grumps is quite far out already, when Sumac looks for him — way past where Sic and Catalpa and Wood have made up some game that involves shoving each other out of the kayak. *Let him go, let him go*, she sings in her head to that earworm of a tune.

"I a egg salad swimmer," crows Brian, clinging to Maxi-Mum's wrist.

"Yes you are. Why don't you show us how you float on your back now?"

And Sumac is relieved, because that means Brian's mouth stays out of the water for a while.

Later, back on the beach, Brian excavates sand and mutters about dinosaurs beside PopCorn, who's putting sticky notes in the margins of a book called *Preschool Art: It's the Process, Not the Product.*

Sumac scans the horizon again, with the binoculars this time.

PopCorn looks up. "Now is that a great black-backed or a lesser black-backed?"

"Greater or lesser what — whale?" she asks, excited.

"Gull."

"Oh." Sumac leans against him. "Is *mislaid* when you can't find something yet but it's not officially lost?"

"Why, what have you mislaid?"

"Your dad," she admits. "I thought he was that speck, but now I think it's just a gull."

"Don't fret, sweet patoot. He'll be out there somewhere."

"But I'm supposed to be his guide dog!" Just two days till the thirty-first; if it's really only two more days, Sumac can manage this. She takes a breath to ask PopCorn if it's true what Grumps said, then lets it out again, because if it's not true, she doesn't want to know.

A small giggle from her father. "Do you think my dad's making a break for it, trying to get to New York State?"

"Technically possible," says MaxiMum from behind her *Advanced Sudoku and Kakuro*. "Remember that girl in the nineteen fifties who swam it in twenty hours and fifty-nine minutes?"

Sumac imagines being that girl: Taking a last desperate glance at her watch — did they have waterproof watches back then, though? — and deciding, *I* will *reach the shore before the twenty-one hours are up.*

PopCorn makes his eyes bulge. "Sumac, you've lost a senior citizen across an international border!"

"Don't tease."

"Impossible. To paraphrase Emma Goldman on dancing — if I can't tease, I don't want to be part of this family." He strokes Sumac's wet hair. "Excellent guide doggy."

"Egg *salad*," Brian corrects him without looking up from her archaeological dig.

Sumac would rather be a guard dog than a guide dog. Her job would be to bark at cranky strangers and keep them away from her family. (Family, as in, the people she actually cares about.)

Wood walks up and flings himself down, like an effigy on the grave of some knight.

"Dad's a hardy old codger," says PopCorn, his eyes on the horizon. "Used to drag me into our local lake the minute it thawed in May," he adds with a shudder. "April, even — he'd bring along a hatchet and smash us a swimming hole."

"Liar liar," sings Aspen.

"Pants on fire," adds Brian.

Catalpa's back now too, reading a graphic novel of *Les Misérables*, with her music on as well.

Waiting for Grumps to reappear is like watching a pot that'll never boil, so Sumac curls up on the sand, letting the sun soak into her shoulder blades. She's at her favorite part of *Pippi Longstocking*, when Pippi buys thirty-six pounds of candy to share with the other kids.

"How's the ancient Sumerian going?" CardaMom asks her.

"Pretty well," Sumac tells her, sitting up. "I'm doing it on my own because *somebody* dropped out of our One-to-One so it's just a One now," she throws in PopCorn's direction.

"Double mega sorry," he groans.

"It's an orphan tongue," she tells CardaMom, "which means it's special because there aren't any other languages related to it. And nobody really knows how it was pronounced, so you're free to say the words any way you like."

"Then if you time-traveled back," says Aspen, deepening the moat around her sand castle, "nobody would understand you?"

Sumac hadn't thought of that. "Hey, something else

that's cool is that it's got two genders, but they're not male and female, they're human and nonhuman. Also . . ." She tries to remember everything she's been cramming. "Mesopotamians wore stone wigs. And they didn't have to have their ears pierced, because they wore hoops right over their ears. Oh, and if a man needed money, he could sell his wife and children as slaves for three years."

PopCorn hoots. "Those were the days when dads had it good. What real use are you to me if I can't rent you out, Nexts of Kin?"

MaxiMum leans over to tap Catalpa on the shoulder, making her jump. Then she disentangles the earbuds from Catalpa's long hair.

"Don't!"

"You're missing some fascinating history."

"Oh, woe," says Catalpa.

"Be present or begone, my love."

"OK, OK." She puts away her music but reopens her paperback and stretches like a panther, yawning.

"Do you think she could have caught sleeping sickness?" PopCorn asks.

"I'm shattered from getting up so hideously early," Catalpa says without looking up.

She's got a job walking a five-year-old to the girl's Space Camp every morning, and home again in the afternoons.

"Ridiculously easy money, I call it," says Wood, eyes still shut on the sand, "so zip your lip. I don't earn a cent for being an Environmental Steward."

"That's because all you guys do is stand around spraying each other with hoses!"

MaxiMum speaks over them: "Family life of the eastern garter snake, Wood?"

He groans and heaves up on one elbow. "OK. Get this: not monogamous. Like, the opposite of monogamous. First they stop eating for two weeks, to get ready."

"Not how I've ever gotten ready for a date," murmurs CardaMom.

"Then they form a mating ball of one female and up to twenty-five males."

"Twenty-five times ew!" cries Aspen.

"Each to their own," says MaxiMum with a shrug.

Sumac wishes Grumps could hear this. *One male + one female = nature's way, my butt!* She squints at the horizon, but there's still no sign of the old man.

"Then the female goes off to give birth —"

"Lay her eggs," Sumac corrects him.

"I likes eggs," remarks Brian.

"Not eggs, live baby snakes, so nyah!" Wood tells Sumac. "Anything between three and ninety-eight of them. *Bye, Mom,* and they all wriggle off on their own."

"Huh," says MaxiMum. "So the two you saw together the other morning?"

"Unrelated, or maybe siblings who'll never see each other again, and good riddance," Wood says, looking around at his sisters.

"How very different from the home life of our own dear Queen," says PopCorn in a posh falsetto.

"Iain, you're quite the swimmer," says MaxiMum.

Sumac jumps. The old man is right behind them, red-faced and dripping.

A couple with a baby and a toddler hover awkwardly at his side. They turn out to be from Lille, and soon CardaMom's chatting away to them in French about how while they're here they have to visit Montreal, where she lived when she was studying to be a lawyer and then being one.

"I was not lost," Grumps keeps repeating gruffly.

"OK, Dad," says PopCorn, "but they said when you came out of the lake you seemed to have no idea —"

"Getting my bearings, I was. Can I not have a moment to myself without busybodies poking their noses in the wrong end of the stick?"

Sumac frowns, trying to picture that.

"I be a egg salad swimmer," Brian tells him.

"Yeah," says MaxiMum, "no life jacket for Brian today, quite a breakthrough."

Grumps mops himself with his towel.

After all that, thinks Sumac furiously, he doesn't even care.

✱

She's in the Bookery the next afternoon, Googling *symptoms old age*. (She only goes into ugly old Spare Oom to sleep; it's never going to be her real room.) Turns out Grumps was right about a certain number of lost marbles being normal at eighty-two. The list of things you lose — not just marbles but height, teeth, sight, hearing, etc., etc. — even makes her a bit sympathetic. Getting old sucks, big-time.

Then she hears another flush, and all her muscles tense up again. Grumps is showing what he thinks of the Lotterys' yellow/brown policy by flushing every time he even walks past one of the bathrooms. Also, he leaves things in the wrong places just to be annoying, like sabotage: crackers in the refrigerator, sunglasses on Opal's perch, milk jug on the bookshelf so it goes sour. . . .

Books are strewn across the table that PapaDum upcycled from what was once somebody's door: *Fun Home, The Inconvenient Indian, Dementia: The Early Stages. . . .* Aha. Sumac reaches for that one.

The first chapter's called "Ruling Out Other Causes." She flicks through and discovers that a lack of vitamin B12 can make your thinking fuzzy . . . but no, then Grumps would look yellowish and be wheezy and dizzy all the time.

Hydrocephalus, which means water on the brain? No, that would make him walk as if his feet were stuck to the floor and wet his pants a lot. Ick.

Irritability and confusion can be caused by severe dehydration. Yes! That must be it. Sumac slaps the book shut and races downstairs.

She bumps into MaxiMum on the Treadmill Landing. "Grumps doesn't drink water," she bursts out. "He boasted to me that he never touches the stuff!"

"And?"

She stops, troubled by a gap in her own logic. "So how come he's not dead yet?"

MaxiMum laughs.

"It's not funny. He could have *severe dehydration.*"

"What do you think tea's made of? And milk, and juice, and lemonade, and fruit, and vegetables?"

"Oh," says Sumac, feeling dumb.

Going back upstairs, she wishes she'd known the old man years ago so she could tell how his mind used to work, and figure out how holey it is now by comparison. Like, CardaMom, say — if she suddenly resorted to the calculator app on her phone to add up eleven croissants plus tax, you'd know there was something terribly wrong. Whereas

PopCorn would never be able to add the tax onto one item, not even with that giant foot-shaped calculator Brian loves. Which is OK, because no two minds work the same way. For instance, Aspen's is speedy and prone to crashing, like a race car. Sic's chess buddy in Osaka has a word for this: *neuro* something, not neurosis. . . . *Neurodiversity*, that's it: differentness of brains.

Sumac's own mind (which she generally thinks of as a pretty good one) is going in slow and pointless circles today. Not like a race car at all; more like the Zhaos' Poop Cube with burst tires.

But she does have one idea for a brain test she can do on Grumps. Downstairs, she taps on the door that still has an unfaded portion in the shape of the *Sumac's Room* sign.

When his long face appears, she asks, "Would you, ah, would you like to play chess with me?"

"What for?"

"I need to," Sumac improvises. "It's like homework."

Down in Gameville, the old man examines their Greek gods set suspiciously as Sumac's setting up the pieces. On the other side of the wall, in the Orchestra Pit, she can hear Catalpa (on guitar and vocals) and Sic (on piano) doing a cover of that Lorde song Sumac's so tired of.

The chess game only lasts about four minutes before Grumps erupts. "You jumped over my king, you wee pup!"

"But it's allowed," she reminds him, "if the king and the rook haven't —"

"It is on your nelly. Only the knight can jump."

"Which is your nelly?" Sumac stares at the board, suddenly unsure. "We always play it that you're allowed to castle if there's nothing between the rook and the king and —"

"Oh, you always play it that way, do ye?" he interrupts. "Ye Lotterys? Well, that's what the rest of us call cheating."

"Sumac doesn't." Sic leans in the doorway, not smiling, for once. "Even when — you know the way little kids always try and cheat because they want to win? Sumac never has."

The old man snorts.

"She's just not a cheater, OK?" says Sic, louder.

"Then she's an ig — an ig — an ignor — an ignoble who doesn't know the rules of chess."

Sumac's having trouble swallowing.

"Want to play with me instead, Smackeroo?" Sic asks her.

She shakes her head, lifting the board to make a landslide. All the gods and goddesses hurtle into their box as if invading the underworld.

"What kind of animal should you never play cards with?" Aspen sticks her head into Gameville under Sic's arm.

"Zip it, Aspen," he mutters.

"Guess! What kind of animal should you never play cards with?" Aspen looks from face to face.

Sumac rams the lid onto the box.

"A cheetah," cries Aspen. "Get it? Get it?"

"I'm not a cheater!" And Sumac doesn't exactly run out, but she goes a lot faster than walking, because she's not going to burst into tears in front of this horrible old man in case he calls her a crybaby.

✱

While CardaMom and MaxiMum are out doing their weeding shift at the community garden the next afternoon and Catalpa's off rehearsing, PapaDum serves up homemade ice pops on the Derriere. Sumac picks one studded with raspberries and chunks of peach.

"Nice little puff of breeze," he says, stretching, but all Sumac can feel is sticky.

"Most fun thing about today?" PopCorn asks, bouncing Oak on his lap.

"I spotted a peregrine falcon," says Wood.

"Wow!" PopCorn's playing Horsey with Oak now, jogging him along till Oak slides off PopCorn's leg and dangles from it like a monkey.

"More than a hundred people showed up for our Green Your Home info session at the library," says PapaDum.

PopCorn beams at him proudly.

PapaDum's sort of a reformed bad guy, because he used to run huge construction projects that turned fields into strip malls, but now he uses his powers for good.

Aspen pretends to be gutted. "What, that was funner than the time you spent with us?" she asks PapaDum.

"Hey, that's one of the pluses of a four-parent family," says PopCorn. "We each get to spend some time being something other than a dad or mom."

PapaDum grins at Aspen. "But brushing your hair was definitely the most *relaxing* thing I did."

That's the only time Aspen sits still, when PapaDum's getting all her tangles out with what he claims is his magic brush.

"My funnest thing, I guess, was . . . acing my Rules of the Road test!" Sic does a little victory dance in his chair. "Now I've started a program on state-of-the-art defensive driving techniques. Backing up, checking your blind spot —"

Sumac peers into her brother's chocolate-brown eyes. "I didn't know you had a blind spot."

"All drivers do," says PapaDum, jerking his thumb behind him, to the left. "It's the bit you can't see in your mirror."

"Changing lanes, braking smoothly" — Sic's large right sneaker rotates and paws the air — "staggering in traffic . . ."

"When you say a *program*," says PapaDum, "do you mean actual lessons?"

"Well, self-taught," says Sic. "It's virtual driving software."

PopCorn rolls his eyes and slides down in his deck chair.

"But it'd be totally legal for me to practice driving for real if there was an adult beside me," Sic assures him.

"An imaginary adult, like Mario?" asks Wood. "Because there's no real adult who'd let you behind the wheel of an actual car."

"*Given enough time,*" Sic quotes, "*a stream can split a mountain.*"

"Yeah, maybe you'll be driving by the time you're Grumps's age," says Wood.

"Where is he, by the way?" asks PopCorn, looking around.

"Brian took him for a walk in the Ravine," says

PapaDum. "The creek's dry, but . . ." He rubs his beard as their eyes meet.

PopCorn stands up, Oak on his hip. "Maybe we'll go see how they're —"

That's when they hear the wailing, and Brian comes tearing down the Wild in her shorts.

PopCorn tries to be heard over the shrieks. "What's the matter, honey?"

But they can all see the streaky rash on Brian's arms and chest, the red bumps already swelling. Poison ivy! Sumac hisses in sympathy. That's going to turn into weeping blisters.

Grumps strides up the garden behind Brian. "Got the bairn out the minute I could."

"Thanks, Iain," PapaDum tells him. "Hose!"

PopCorn's already running for it. "Have to wash the resin off, Brian, the sticky poison."

She shrieks under the cold water.

"Here, boots off so I can spray your feet," PapaDum's telling Grumps.

"Dad! Your feet," says PopCorn.

"Don't scratch," PapaDum advises the old man, tugging off his steel-capped boots. "The thing is to rinse it off and then sit in a lukewarm bath."

"Let's get your socks into a garbage bag, Dad."

"I'm not throwing out my socks," says Grumps in a shocked tone.

"We just need to wash them."

"Those are perfectly good socks."

"What about yogurt? Or chamomile tea," says PopCorn, yanking off Brian's shorts and underwear. "That can be soothing."

PapaDum snorts. "Hydrocortisone and antihistamines are what they need. I'll check the medicine cabinet."

"Socks, Dad," pleads PopCorn.

"The boy," says Grumps, staring.

"Wood?" says Sumac, looking around.

"The wee baldy one." Grumps is pointing at naked Brian, who's shuddering under the hose. "He's a girl."

A silence, which Brian breaks. "I not a girl!"

Aspen titters. "Didn't you know?" she asks Grumps.

He gives her a fierce look.

Sumac's staggered. How can the man have spent nearly two weeks here thinking Brian's a boy?

"At the moment, Brian's preferring not to be called that," murmurs PopCorn.

The stubbled ridges where Grumps's eyebrows are starting to grow back go up. "Not to be called a girl?"

"*Not* a girl," shrieks Brian.

But then again, Sumac realizes, the Lotterys are a big mob, and they talk a lot and often all at the same time. Grumps must have heard *she* sometimes, but not known that it was this particular bald four-year-old being talked about.

"Why did you name her Brian, for the love of God?" he demands.

"It was actually Briar," says Sumac, "but she changed it when she was three."

"Ye are all out of your tiny minds," says Grumps, and stomps away to the house in his dripping socks.

✱

After the moms get back, Wood proposes a game in the Ravine called Friend or Foe, so that nobody else will get hurt this summer. (Grumps doesn't answer when Aspen knocks on his door to ask if he wants to come along.)

Wood points to a jagged leaf.

"Nettle, foe," shouts Brian. She can't reach her shins to scratch her rashes because she's got her fire truck on, so she rubs them against a tree.

"Mm, what's this delicious little friend?" asks Sic, leaning over some orange globes.

"Let me taste." Aspen reaches for one.

"Foe! You're so dead," Wood tells her. "That's Jerusalem cherry."

"Aspen not dead," says Brian, a little uncertainly.

"This one's a strawberry, totally friendly," Sumac tells her, swallowing one.

"Who's the leader of this game?" demands Wood.

"It's not a military expedition," murmurs CardaMom.

"This is life-or-death stuff, Mother."

"Whoops, should I have pretended she didn't know a strawberry when she saw one?" asks Sumac.

"*I* wants strawberry," says Brian.

"And what in the world could that one be?" asks Aspen, wide-eyed. "It's black and it's a berry. . . ." She drops it in Brian's palm. "Could it just ever so possibly be our friend blackberry?"

"Don't want blackberry." Brian hurls it back in the bush.

"I'd have eaten that," Sumac complains.

"I want strawberry!" Brian bangs on the cardboard sides of her truck.

"Stay calm if you want to stay with the gang," CardaMom reminds her. "What about elderberry?" She points to a small dark fruit.

"Don't tell this loser crew the names," Wood rebukes her. "They need to know the plants by sight, for survival."

"You mean in the End Times?" asks Sic, sniggering. "When you, with all your *wood lore*, rise to be boy leader of the handful of Torontonians left alive?"

187

Wood aims a karate kick at him, but Sic jumps away.

"You mock your little brother now," says PopCorn to Sic, "but come the Apocalypse, you'll be begging to get into his fortified compound."

"So is elderberry a friend or foe?" asks Sumac.

CardaMom makes a *kinda* gesture with her hand. "Like beans, it turns friendly when you cook it."

They're heading down the slope of the Ravine now. The path's still a bit crumbly from the flash floods earlier in the summer. "Leaf of three, let it be," chants Brian balefully, waggling her finger at some low green leaves with red berries.

"Actually, that one's a friend called fragrant sumac," MaxiMum tells her. "See, the three stems are all the same length. With poison ivy the middle one's longer."

Brian scratches one of her bumpy legs with her other foot. "Leaf of three be my foe!"

Her little sister does recognize leafs of three, Sumac thinks with a cold sensation. Could Brian have run into the poison ivy to save Grumps, not vice versa?

"Anyone remember how to tell poison sumac from fragrant?" asks MaxiMum.

"White fruit that sticks up," Wood tells the group.

"White, yeah, but it dangles down." MaxiMum makes her hands droop and puts on a monster face.

Sumac feels a tiny stab of pleasure at the sight of Wood's expression.

"By the way, young ones," says CardaMom as they head back up toward their property line, "new rules."

"How many new rules, and for what?" Sumac pulls her notepad out of her shorts to take them down.

"Just one. Your grandfather's not able to be in charge of the little ones," says MaxiMum, "so if Brian's with him, or Oak, a teenager or an adult needs to be there too."

"Does it matter?" asks Sumac.

Everyone stares, and she feels herself turning red. "I only mean, if he might be going tomorrow, or whenever the results come in —"

"Going where?" asks MaxiMum.

"Like, leaving," says Sumac, faltering. "Back to Faro."

PopCorn says, in a hoarse voice, "Cherub, my dad's never going back to Faro."

What, *never*? How can they be sure of that? Sumac blinks. "But he said *you* said, two weeks and you'd see. Two weeks is the last day of July; that's tomorrow."

"I don't think anybody would have said anything as specific as two weeks," CardaMom tells her.

"*A couple of weeks*, then," Sumac growls. "He marked it on his calendar. The flower calendar in his room, with the circle around the date?"

Blank looks all around.

"You're the best noticer in the family," says CardaMom.

"He said he was perfectly *minty*" — Sumac suddenly can't retrieve the phrase — "some Latin words that mean perfectly solid in his mind, and it'd all been a big mistake."

"If you're such a good noticer," scoffs Wood, "how come you haven't noticed the guy's brains are fried?"

"Wood," protests CardaMom.

"Scrambled!" He mimes whipping eggs. "He put his sunglasses in the microwave."

"Did he cook them?" asks PopCorn, horrified.

Wood shakes his head. "I stopped him just in time."

"He can still play chess," Sumac argues confusedly.

"Did he win, though?" says Sic.

"He — we stopped the game because he called me a cheater. He plays by different rules." Even as Sumac says it, she can hear what it sounds like: bogus.

"Meaning, he's forgotten the rules," says MaxiMum. "I'm sorry, Sumac, but his test results are all back, and they show a lot of cognitive deficits. Gaps," she says. (For once, without telling the kids to *look it up*.)

"He doesn't remember who the prime minister is," says PopCorn miserably.

"Who cares?" says Aspen. "I don't know that."

"Me neither," says Sumac. That's a lie, actually. Of course Sumac knows who the boss of Canada is, but most nine-year-olds wouldn't. Like, at the playground the other day, Isabella and Liam were sure it was Barack Obama.

"Will his brain bits grow back, like his eyebrows?" Aspen asks.

The parents all look at each other, then shake their heads.

A tear runs down Sumac's cheek, startling her. It's not about Grumps. It's because this whole summer's down the toilet, and she wishes it was over already.

CHAPTER 9

ACCOMMODATION

The next day, the one marked on Grumps's calendar, the parents have a record-breakingly long Dull Conversation — around the Trampoline, so Oak can entertain himself by rolling around on it. Then the moms go around the corner to grab falafel and bring it back for lunch while the dads explain the situation to the old man.

Sumac is huddled on the stairs with all her siblings, listening to the fight in the Grumpery. There's nothing dormant about their grandfather anymore: He's an erupting volcano now, spewing out gas and ash and lava in all directions. "Robbers," he roars.

Oak is practicing stairs. He prefers to crawl down rather than up, because then gravity's his friend, but he hasn't factored in the face-plants, so his sibs keep having to scoop him up at the last minute and flip him around so he's heading upward again. Luckily he finds this funny rather than annoying.

"Abductors!" screeches the old man.

"LOL," Opal screams from the Mess. "LOL!"

Sumac feels so sick, she doesn't think she'll be able to manage any falafel.

"Where the doctors?" asks Brian puzzledly.

"Abductors," Sic tells her.

"Like, kidnappers," says Wood.

Brian's eyes cross slightly. "Where the kidnappers?"

It's too hard to explain, so nobody does.

"What if the neighbors call the police?" asks Aspen.

Catalpa groans. "I bet it was Mrs. Zhao who phoned Social Services last year because of your bruises."

That was the most embarrassing moment of Sumac's life so far, when the social worker turned up to ask how Aspen had got so many *aspendents*.

"Ye take my car away," Grumps thunders now, "hustle me onto a plane, trap me in this weirdy commune! Elder abuse, that's what it is."

"Poor Grumps," murmurs Catalpa.

Sumac scowls at her. Wasn't her big sister the one who objected most loudly to the dads and moms *shipping in some random old guy* in the first place? So why is Catalpa posing as all nicey-nicey now?

PopCorn's voice, from the Grumpery: "Dad, do you remember what the doctor said about —"

"You," the old man interrupts, "sitting in judgment on my sanity, I like that! All daubed with tattoos, with your oddball lifestyle and your pack of mongrels —"

"Don't speak to your son that way!"

The kids all stiffen because that's PapaDum, sounding angrier than they've ever heard him.

Oak lets out a squeak. Sic blows little raspberries on his head.

PopCorn's professional counselor voice, all low and lulling; Sumac can't make out what he's saying.

"But we've only got one mongrel, that's Diamond. She's not a pack," says Aspen. "Maybe Grumps thinks Kipper from the apartment building is ours? But he's nearly all yellow Labrador."

"Us," hisses Sumac. "We're the mongrels."

"Don't sweat it," says Sic with a shrug. "Mutts make the best dogs."

"But —"

"It's a fact: We're a raggle-taggle, multiculti crew. Grumps was raised on racism, homophobia, all that jazz. Nineteen thirties ring a bell at all? Hitler? Ex-ter-min-ate!" Sic adds in a robotic voice.

But Sumac's seen ninety-year-olds boogieing on floats in the Pride Parade. "Yeah, well, he's had decades and decades to grow out of being like that. At this rate he'll still be narrow-minded when he's a hundred."

Silence falls as the kids consider that.

"I'm so hungry I could eat my own fist," says Wood.

"I'll run down the street and see if they're coming," offers Aspen.

"Sh," says Sumac, listening hard, because the voices in the Grumpery are rising again.

"We've taken you in, Iain," PapaDum's saying, "and in return, you could have the common courtesy to —"

"Who asked you to take me in, Saint Gandhi?" roars Grumps. "Didn't want to be taken in, did I? Wanted to stay right where I was!"

And then the front door scrapes open and MaxiMum calls up, "Lunch," so the kids all clatter down the stairs, Wood lugging Oak over his shoulder, firefighter-style.

*

Grumps spends all Wednesday and Thursday in his room, giving the Lotterys the silent treatment. He still gets on Sumac's nerves even when he's out of sight.

On Friday morning, she and Aspen are down in the Saw Pit making a meter-wide mud, twig, and pebble model of Toronto in 1954. Of course Sumac's doing most of the work, but Aspen can concentrate on things surprisingly well if they're morbid or disgusting. Once his sisters are done, Wood's promised to help them re-create Hurricane Hazel and the flood that killed eighty-one people across the city.

When the whine of a drill cuts through the air, Sumac follows it upstairs to the Grumpery, where she finds PapaDum up a stepladder drilling a hole in the ceiling. Their grandfather isn't there, but the room has his musty oldie smell. His cases have disappeared, which gets Sumac excited for a minute, but then she figures out that he must have unpacked them.

"Is he . . ." She stops herself from saying *gone*, because that's just wishful thinking. "Out?"

PapaDum nods. "PopCorn took him to the shoe store for orthotics to make his feet comfier."

Why doesn't Grumps just swap his steel-toe boots for sandals, Sumac wonders? "What are you doing?"

196

"Putting an exhaust fan in the ceiling to suck smoke out."

"But smoking's against the rules."

A sigh. "Well, this would be what's called an accommodation, *beta*."

That confuses her. "Isn't the whole house an accommodation, because people live in it?"

"The word also means making space for someone." The drill screams, then PapaDum goes on: "Bending a rule, meeting halfway, splitting the difference."

"So Grumps is allowed to smoke now?" Sumac asks, squeaky with outrage.

"The fan should keep it from spreading."

Accommodation means that you cave, basically. (Like giving Brian chocolate mousse after she's had a tantrum and banged her head on the table.) *Splitting the difference*, so nobody's going to be happy: The Lotterys would rather not have foul toxins leaking through their house, and Grumps would prefer to live somewhere he could smoke whenever he liked.

And then Sumac's pulse starts speeding up, because she's had a stroke of genius.

Places where he might be happier, MaxiMum said, meaning one of those *homes* that are like orphanages for oldies. CardaMom called it *being looked after by strangers* instead of *his people*, but that hasn't worked out, has it, because

Grumps thinks of the Lotterys as *weirdy abductors*, not *his people* at all.

So Sumac doesn't need to change her parents' minds. All she has to do is get Grumps to say that if he's not allowed to go back to Yukon, he'd rather live in one of those *homes*, where he'll be at least a bit happier, because the other orphan oldies will probably flush the toilet every time.

She hears a commotion, so she hurries out into the Hall of Mirrors. CardaMom — Oak in her arms — is supervising on the stairs while Aspen sweeps up broken glass. "Brian, not with your hands!"

"I helping," says Brian.

"Hold the brush pan steady for Aspen," says CardaMom. "That's helping."

The front door opens and PopCorn steps in, followed by his father. "What's all the hullabaloo?"

"Some wineglasses smashed their selves by accident," Aspen tells him.

"Not how it was," says CardaMom.

"I was doing a physics experiment to see if gravity would make the water wick from one glass to another all down the stairs, but then Slate tickled me, so I tripped over the yarn." Slate's head pops out of Aspen's collar.

Grumps gives the whole scene a disgusted glare.

All this chaos is splendid, Sumac decides. The more the old man is appalled by life at Camelottery, the easier it'll be to persuade him to demand to move out. She sidles over and says, almost in his ear, "Sometimes she sings the same jingle for" — half an hour? hours? — "*days* on end."

The old man jumps. "Who?"

"Aspen." Sumac points, in case he's forgotten which girl is which. "She doesn't even notice when she picks her nose and wipes it on the wall."

"I don't care for tattling, Little Miss Perfect."

Sumac is stung. "I didn't mean — I mean, we've all got faults," she stammers. "Wood teaches the parrot filthy words, and Sic's feet stink like you wouldn't believe, and Catalpa's bone idle, and I'm" — she tries to pick just one of the things her siblings have accused her of — "I can be a pompous smart-ass."

Grumps lets out a snort.

She doesn't mean to amuse him. This is deadly serious. "It must be pretty hideous, living with us instead of on your own," she says. "I mean, we're used to us and don't know any different, but even we get bugged by us."

"I didn't do it on purpose," Aspen's repeating cheerfully.

"In between accident and purpose there's a gray area called negligence," says CardaMom in her lawyer voice.

"What's —"

"Carelessness, Aspen Elspeth!" says PopCorn, trying to be funny and not quite pulling it off.

Grumps turns on him. "Your mother Elspeth?"

"Aspen Elspeth Aspen Elspeth Aspen Elspeth," says Aspen like a fast and spitty tongue twister. "Catalpa has our aunty Ajesh for her middle, and Wood has Michael from a dead friend of PapaDum's, and Sic has Tecumseh, who captured Detroit."

"I'm Portia from a Shakespeare play and also the prime minister of Jamaica," Sumac adds, "and Brian has Bree and Oak has Owen, because those were the names their birth mom gave them."

Grumps ignores all that and scowls at Aspen. "This child never even met Elspeth."

"That's right, Dad, and that's sad," says PopCorn.

The silence lengthens. You'd think the old man would be glad that somebody remembers his wife enough to pass on her name thirty years later, thinks Sumac. But no, Grumps behaves as if it's one more thing stolen from him. When he's the robber, actually. The Lotterys were in a jar, like treasure in ancient Mesopotamia, and he's barged his way in and cracked the seal off.

Sumac steps over the shards of glass and marches all the way up to her new room. (Her cell of exile, more like.) In

200

big capitals she starts a list of what kind of *home* would suit her grandfather.

NOBODY WITH TATTOOS

NO WHOLE GRAINS OR "FOREIGN VEGETABLES"

NO NOSEY PARKERS

NO GRUBBING ABOUT IN GARBAGE

NO HAVING TO TAKE PILLS

NO BEING NAGGED OR BOSSED AROUND

NO CRIPPLED ANIMALS

NOBODY UNDER 18

Is it all a bit negative? Well, that's because Grumps is.

Sumac tries to think of positive things that would make one of those *homes* homier to him than Camelottery is. Does disliking children mean Grumps is fond of old people, or not necessarily? Most things she knows he likes — cups of tea, shortbread, easy crosswords, classical music — he can get here. What can't he? *Peace and quiet*, she adds to her list.

WILDFLOWERS OF YUKON

WHITE BREAD

WHITE PASTA

ALL WHITE PEOPLE

Sumac can't quite imagine anywhere that's like that nowadays. Maybe what Grumps needs is a time machine — only then he wouldn't ask to go to an old folks' home, would he? He'd aim straight for his real home in Faro, but thirty years back, when Elspeth was alive. No, actually, more like forty or fifty years, so he could have enough time with her before she'd die again.

Now Sumac's feeling sorry for him. Grrr. She has to stay focused. It's like her grandfather's a miserable beluga, and Sumac needs to find him a new pod to join. Or no, she's still his guide dog, but her job is to guide him in a direction that's truly best for him by giving him little nudges.

She starts looking up websites. It's even harder than ancient Sumerian, trying to figure out the differences between *independent living* and *adult living* and *assisted living*. She has to admit, one good thing about having a bedroom in the attic is privacy: Nobody wanders in and interrupts her here.

Until MaxiMum knocks on the door to say that's enough screen time, and by the way, Aspen got bored waiting for Sumac to come back and finish their model, so she tinkered with history by destroying Toronto with a massive meteor strike.

✱

Why do the Lotterys never seem to get around to going to the playground till it's the hottest part of the afternoon, Sumac wonders?

In the Hall of Mirrors, they pass Sic loading up his tool belt with compound, spring clips, and pliers.

"Got putty knives?" PapaDum asks.

"Flexible and stiff," says Sic, whipping them out ninja-style. Today's home-printed T-shirt says *Back to Front*.

Sumac peeks behind him to see what the back says. In upside-down letters, *This Way Up*. "What's your project?"

"Glazing Mrs. Zhao's window that me and Wood cracked this morning playing one-armed basketball," he tells her.

She winces sympathetically.

"Don't just carry those safety goggles," says PapaDum, "wear them."

"You have taught me well, Obi-Wan Kenobi." Sic bows deeply. "Now I set forth on my perilous journey to the land of Zhao. . . ."

The playground's only five minutes away, but Sumac feels more than half melted already.

PopCorn starts rigging up his latest great idea — a slackline between two trees, knee-high, so if you fall, it won't hurt too much. He pads the loops with Bubble Wrap to avoid damaging the bark.

"Keep it horizontal while I ratchet it tighter," calls CardaMom.

"It is horizontal," insists PopCorn. "It just looks slanty to you because you're bent over."

She broods over the diagram in the booklet and lets out a grunt of frustration.

PopCorn straightens up and twangs the tight nylon ribbon between the two trees. "Ready as it'll ever be."

"Take baby steps," CardaMom reads aloud.

"Huh! I've walked walls five times higher than this." Catalpa puts one bare foot on the line and straightens up, as graceful as an acrobat. Then she steps forward . . . and gets thrown off, landing on her chin in the grass.

Sumac gnaws her lips to keep her laugh inside.

"I go, I go," shouts Brian.

PopCorn persuades Brian to hold his hand, just for her first turn, so she manages to walk the entire length of the line.

Aspen scampers for about three steps before she boings off, lands askew, and announces in a stoic voice that she's broken her ankle — which everybody ignores.

Sumac tries what the leaflet recommends, which is standing still on one leg on the slackline, staring at a fixed point ahead of you.

"My go again already," calls Aspen.

"No it's not."

"You're not even moving."

"I'm getting my balance," says Sumac, barely moving her lips.

"Can I walk from the other end, as you're not using it?"

"No!" Sumac leans a little forward . . . but the line heaves sideways, and she has to step down onto the grass.

"A score of zero centimeters for Sumac Lottery, a record-breaking fail," crows Aspen.

"That's called a controlled dismount," Sumac tells her.

She wishes Wood had come today so she could talk to him about her secret plan to make Grumps demand to leave Camelottery, but — too cool, at twelve — he says playgrounds are for children. She's tempted to try Brian, but four-year-olds are horribly honest, so Brian might well blab about it to the parents, or Grumps himself, even.

Instead, Sumac goes to crouch down beside Catalpa and says softly, "Hey. I have an idea for getting —" She stops herself, because *getting rid of* sounds mean. "For getting Grumps to move out, persuading him to ask to go, you know?" She waits for her sister's reaction. Then finally realizes that Catalpa has her earbuds in. She taps one black-draped arm.

Catalpa jumps as if Sumac's stabbed her and pauses her music. "What?" She interrupts before Sumac's more than half explained it. "Oh, leave the guy alone."

"You said it was totally not democratic to move him in!"

"That was weeks ago. He's not doing anyone any harm."

Easy for Catalpa to say, when she's out most of the time with her *bandmates*, and she didn't have to give up her Turret.

"Get a life," she says, covering a yawn with one black-nailed hand and turning her music back on.

Not for the first time, Sumac moves Catalpa down the list of family members to Least Favorite. Well, she's still above Grumps, but he doesn't count.

Sumac squints at the slackline, where Aspen's managed four steps in a row. Nobody can teach Aspen anything, but sometimes she teaches herself things in a blink. Whereas

Sumac prefers the kind of lesson that doesn't leave twigs embedded in her shins.

MaxiMum falls heavily and takes a long breath before she gets up and brushes off her shorts. *"Fall down seven times,"* she quotes, *"get up eight."*

Sumac frowns. "That doesn't make any sense," she calls. "If you fall down seven times, you only need to get up seven."

"Zen mind, very mysterious," says PopCorn. "Sound of one hand clapping. What face you have before father and mother born?"

"What does that even mean?" asks Sumac.

"He has no idea," MaxiMum tells her.

"What is sound one father blah-blahing, no one listening?" asks Aspen, hurdling over the slackline and back again.

Sumac beckons her sister over for a quiet chat behind a tree.

Aspen is much more appreciative of Sumac's plan than Catalpa was. "Let's dress up in sheets and convince him Camelottery's haunted!"

"Don't be ridiculous, that's too *Scooby-Doo.*"

"I could set off fireworks under his bed. . . ."

"Nothing life-threatening," Sumac tells her sternly. "And whatever you do, don't tell the parents till I've found a really good home that he'll want to move into. Not Sic either," she adds, struck by an uncomfortable feeling that her beloved eldest brother might not understand that Sumac's doing all this for Grumps's good.

"Top secret," says Aspen, zipping her lip ferociously. "Hey, I could go stand right beside Grumps whenever I feel a fart coming. Or maybe I'll sneak Slate into his room and blow his mind with terror! And we could put apple pie in his bed like in the old books."

Sumac gets called for her next turn before she has a chance to explain that apple pie beds just had the sheets tucked so you couldn't straighten your legs; there was no actual pie in them.

She manages one step on the slackline before she's flung sideways. "Argh! This is a dud line."

"No, it's wonderful, we're learning so much," says CardaMom, picking a bit of beechnut shell out of her elbow.

"You mean we're humiliating ourselves in front of the entire neighborhood yet again," complains Catalpa.

It's true, the slackline has drawn kids like the tinkle of an ice cream truck. Even a cluster of old people with those sticks with claws at the bottom. A tiny boy hovers.

"Want a turn?" PopCorn asks him, with a gracious sweep of the hand like he's Sir Walter Raleigh greeting Queen Elizabeth.

The child scampers along the rope as if it's a streak of chalk.

"Now that's what I'm talking about!" PopCorn starts clapping, so the sulking Lottery kids have to join in.

"I think it needs to be slacker," says MaxiMum.

"Tighter," says PapaDum, who's just arrived. Oak crawls underneath the line, dribbling contentedly.

Sumac's mood sinks at the sight of Grumps behind the newcomers. The old man parks himself on the farthest bench, as if he doesn't know the Lotterys.

But the more ashamed of them he is, the better for Sumac's secret plan. . . .

She sidles over and sits on the bench, but not right beside him. "We do these kinds of bizarro things in public all the time."

He shoots her a sidelong glance, and she squirms.

In the distance, PopCorn's got his shirt off as he wrestles with the slackline. With his buzzed hair and his faded tats, he could almost strike you as scary if you didn't know what a pussycat he is. "Did you know your son's got eleven tattoos in total?" asks Sumac. "The four elements — that's fire on the back of his neck, but most of the orange is sunburned off, and a crescent moon on his left knee, see? And the rising sun on his right one. . . ."

"Saints preserve us," murmurs Grumps. This is working like a charm. "He has an arm sleeve on his right, that's a Japanese koi morphing into a dragon. There's — lots of hearts with the names of his ex-boyfriends in," Sumac adds, stretching a point because actually there's just one. "Oh, and that monster on PopCorn's lower back, that's about accepting his dark side. Betty Boop on his tummy, but she's gone a bit shapeless, because apparently you should never put a tattoo anywhere that's going to get baggy. Also, the black lines on his right calf are one of Ötzi's tattoos. Ötzi's a five-thousand-year-old mummy in the Alps with sixty-one tattoos."

Grumps's gummy eyes are wide, appalled.

Brian is at Sumac's elbow. "What?" she asks impatiently.

The small hand uncurls just a little.

"It's all dark in there." Sumac pries her sister's grubby fingers a little farther open. A wink of blue.

"I finded it in the sand but not for Gneiss Nilda," says Brian. "I have it for me."

Anything in the playground that isn't somebody's gets left on the memorial rock of Nilda, a girl from the nearby apartments who only lived to be two and a half. The rock is the kind called gneiss, which sounds like *nice*, so the kids all call her Gneiss Nilda.

"But maybe it *his's*," says Brian, nodding at their grandfather.

Sumac feels irritated and softened at the same time. "No — that was just — his brains aren't actual marbles that he's lost, remember," she says in Brian's ear, "they're just *like* marbles."

Brian shakes her head as if her big sister is being particularly stupid. "Better give it back."

"But, Brian —"

She strokes the glass with one dirty finger, then edges past Sumac to Grumps. The neck emerging from the red cardboard truck looks so small. Please don't let him bite her head off, thinks Sumac.

Brian holds out her hand flat with the marble on it.

Grumps picks it up. "Ah, a nice wee blue Swirly. When they're that small they're called peewees, really. I had any number of them. Commies, Toothpastes, Turtles, Oilies . . . one big boss Devil's Eye. Couple of Bumblebees. Never cared for Opaques. Bloods were my favorite, or Green Ghosts."

Sumac has never heard the man say so much at one time.

"Legendary, my collection was. Whatever happened to it?"

"You loseded them," Brian reminds him.

Grumps revolves the little ball between his big flat fingers. "We used to trade. Or play Bools, where you try to smash the other boys' taws."

"This only one," says Brian. "What you do with one?"

"There was a game called Poison with four holes. . . . Let's keep it simple, start with one hole."

"Too hard for a hole," Brian objects.

"No, no, a hole in something else, for the marble to roll into. Here, this'll do in a pinch," says Grumps, picking a polystyrene cup out of the trash can and digging his fingernail into the rim.

He's playing, thinks Sumac in disbelief. And with garbage!

✱

By the next morning she's wishing she never opened her mouth to Aspen. Honestly, if Aspen had been in on the plot to murder Julius Caesar, she'd have gathered the plotters on the wrong street on the wrong day, with kites instead of knives.

At breakfast, for instance, Aspen sets down a bowl in front of Grumps with a smile like a smarmy waiter's and a wink at Sumac. "Your favorite cereal, m'lud, with a little something special."

Sumac snatches the bowl just as Grumps puts his spoon into it. The spoon flies across the table and clangs on the tiles, splashing milk.

Everybody stares.

"Sorry," she cries. "It, ah, it had a bit of dried food stuck to the rim."

"Wouldn't bother me," says Grumps with a snort.

But Sumac's running to the garbage to empty the bowl already, and find a new one, and fill that with cereal herself, and wipe up the floor.

When Grumps is halfway through his breakfast, Sumac hisses in Aspen's ear, "What was the *something special?*"

"Only a little sprinkle from the sandbox," whispers Aspen.

Sumac pokes her in the shoulder.

Aspen pokes her even harder, in the solar plexus, so Sumac doubles over. "Sand wouldn't kill him unless he ate kilos of the stuff!"

"No more poisoning!" whispers Sumac, right in Aspen's face.

"Could you two behave yourselves or leave the table?" asks MaxiMum.

"I'm done anyway," says Aspen, who's only had a couple of bites of her breakfast sandwich. She uses her plate to juggle her crusts all the way to the sink.

Later that morning Sumac's rounding up the dirty clothes, which is one of her favorite Lots: collecting the bags from outside each bedroom and kicking and rolling them down all the flights to Sock Heaven in the basement.

She hears balls clacking in Gameville and puts her head in to find Aspen playing a game she calls Ricochet, which is pool without cues.

"Superglue," sings Aspen.

"What about it?" asks Sumac. "Have you made yourself a fumb again?"

Aspen draws a big rectangle in the air. Then mimes trying to open a door handle, and frowning, and struggling.

"You didn't!"

"It's guaranteed to annoy him," Aspen assures her.

"Which door?" asks Sumac desperately.

"Duh, Grumps's."

"Is he in his room or out of it?"

As if answering her come two massive thumps from the

ground floor, above them, and then the bang of a door against a wall.

"Out, now, I guess," says Aspen, disappointed. "The old guy's got a kick like a mule."

"No more clever ideas," Sumac pleads with her. Then scurries back to Sock Heaven to busy herself filling the second washing machine, so she can pretend she had nothing to do with it.

"Only if they're *ultra* clever ones," Aspen calls through the wall.

But nobody comes looking for Sumac, and the cowbell doesn't ring, nor the police whistle (which is for family emergencies). Grumps must not have complained to any of the parents about his door being stuck shut. Maybe he thinks that's just something that happens in a hundred-and-thirty-year-old house?

When Sumac passes the Grumpery a little later, the door is ajar; you'd never notice the little shiny line of glue unless you were looking for it.

More than one voice inside. "No bigger than your three-legged friend there —"

Does he mean Diamond? She puts her head in.

"— but this fella could kill a deer nonetheless," says Grumps.

"Seriously?" asks Wood. He and his dog are peering into one of a set of huge boxes full of packing beads, which take up nearly the entire floor.

"No bother to him. There was one up north, suffocated a polar bear by biting his throat."

"But a polar bear, that's like ten times the size. Twenty. No *way*." Wood says it as if he wants to believe it. He's lifting something out of the beads now.

A head! Sumac recoils. Stuffed, glass-eyed. A terrible animal muzzle with a faint mask of silvery hair. Wood is grinning at it, nose to nose.

As Grumps bangs a hook into the wall — *her* blue-sky wall, that's how Sumac still thinks of it — it releases a little shower of old plaster. Should someone with Swiss cheese for brains be allowed a hammer, she wonders? "Is that a, uh, some kind of bear?" she asks, troubled that she doesn't know.

Grumps blinks at her. "Who invited you in, missy?"

Her throat locks. "I was just asking. *There are no stupid questions*," she quotes.

He snorts as if he doesn't agree. "It's a wolverine," he says, taking the horrible head from Wood and hanging it on the wall.

Diamond barks at it fiercely.

Sumac frowns. Aren't wolverines endangered or something?

"Got a special sideways tooth in the back there, meant for tearing into frozen carrion," says Grumps.

Wood sticks his finger into the dark maw. "Sharp!"

"Wouldn't have been much use if it wasn't," says Grumps.

"Is it related to a wolf?" asks Sumac.

"More like a, a, a whatchamacallit," says Grumps, smacking his leg quite hard, as if that'll shake the word loose. "Pardon my tartle."

"Your what?" says Wood.

"Tip of my tongue," says Grumps as if to himself. "Your man here is big brother to the wee fella, long-legged. . . ."

What's *wee* with long legs? Not a spider, obviously. "Greyhound?" suggests Sumac.

"No," he says, scornful. "Sneaky, like. Stealing eggs. Sto, stee, steasel. Weasel," he almost shouts. "A wolverine's a kind of weasel." Tapping it on the muzzle.

"Can I hang up the next one?" asks Wood.

"You can *not*," says Grumps.

"We're all used to power tools from the age of, like, eight," Wood points out.

"Mm, I gather you pick up a couple of practical things along with all the Mesopotamian nonsense."

Sumac's lips tighten.

Grumps fits a nail into the next hook, fingers fumbling slightly, and hammers it into the wall with three clean taps. He pulls a skull with elaborate curly horns out of the next box and fits it on the hook. "One of the famous mountain sheep of Faro."

What kind of monster slaughters sheep for a hobby, thinks Sumac? He's turning her lovely room into a tomb.

"I'm really psyched to go hunting sometime," says Wood, lifting up a caribou head. "But the folks are all wary of anything more than a Nerf gun. . . ."

"Your father's not a bad shot."

"PopCorn?" says Sumac, appalled.

"You're kidding," says Wood.

"This was back before anyone was *vegetarian*," Grumps adds with scorn.

"Hey, you want to come batting with us this evening?" asks Wood.

"I was more of a footie player in my time."

"No, not baseball — bat watching. In High Park, around sunset." And Wood goes off on how the Urban Bat Project crowdsources data by training teens like him as rangers, blah blah blah blah blah, and what's really getting on Sumac's nerves is how buddy-buddy her brother's being with the enemy all of a sudden. She's been waiting for the

right moment to ask Wood to help with her secret plan to get Grumps out of Camelottery, but now it looks like she's too late.

Nuzu egalla bacar, she recites in her head. Ignoramuses are horribly numerous in this palace.

CHAPTER 10

MARBLES

Even when the Lotterys do their usual summer things, these days, Sumac enjoys them about 75 percent less because of Grumps pooh-poohing them. At the Chinatown Festival, for instance, he sits on a bench ("too hard") doing a crossword ("too easy") and picking at his chicken cashew nut ("too spicy") instead of coming along on a produce hunt. (The kids' triple challenge is to find and buy a golden dragon fruit, an ice cream fruit — called that because when it's chilled it tastes kind of like bubble gum — and a spiky, stinky durian.) Grumps barely even glances up to watch the thirty-meter dragon dance by in the parade. What would it take to please him?

On Monday half the family are going to Toytally Awesome to buy presents for Oak's birthday. Brian's allowed to wear her fire truck as long as she leaves it outside the store so she won't knock stuff down with it. "I *drive* it to toy store and *park* outside," she says.

"What I meant, obviously," says CardaMom.

They're waiting on the doorstep for Sic, who can't find socks that don't match. "He always has to have odd socks," Sumac explains to Grumps, because that's something else he might find *weirdy*. "And Aspen turns her underwear inside out, and —"

"Shut up," Aspen roars, pink-faced. "It's so the label won't rub."

Today Aspen's T-shirt is both backward and inside out, Sumac notices. "And Catalpa will only wear gothy punky black stuff," she goes on, "and Brian always picks boy clothes, of course. Did you see CardaMom's ribbon dress when she was going to the Gala Gathering the other evening, and her beaded collar?"

"What are you all of a sudden," sneers Catalpa, "some tween fashion blogger?"

MaxiMum is giving Sumac a curious look.

"Come *on*, Sic," calls PopCorn. "I may only have another forty years to live!"

Aspen puts her head into the Hall of Mirrors and shrieks, "Put one of your socks inside out so it'll be a different texture!"

Finally Sic thumps down the stairs and vaults over the last baby gate, one sock inside out.

"Why can't you just wear sandals?" asks PopCorn, wriggling his own hairy toes.

Pulling on his sneakers, Sic shakes his head. "Don't go there, old man. If I have to start explaining the philosophy behind my threads —"

"Can we just get out of here?" asks MaxiMum.

More delay two blocks down the street, because CardaMom can't pass someone who's begging without getting into a long conversation as well as giving them a twenty-dollar bill.

"So Mrs. Zhao thought I was far too young to be using a heat gun on her window," Sic remarks, "but by the time I put the glass in, she seemed to be warming to me. She had the impression all we do is pogo and goof off, so I briefed her on the advanced trig course I'm taking. Know what's in those boxes she's always cramming into the Poop Cube?"

"Mangoes," guesses Aspen randomly.

"Counterfeit money," says Sumac.

"Personalized dolls," Sic tells them.

"Personalized like with names?" asks Sumac, puzzled.

"Like with everything! You send in your kid's photo and Mrs. Zhao cobbles together the right hair, skin, shirt, scans the face right onto the fabric. . . ."

"Sinister," says Catalpa, checking her phone.

"They're selling like hotcakes," he tells her.

Aspen starts "John Jacob Jingleheimer Schmidt" — she likes to sing campfire songs faster and faster as she cat's cradles — but halfway through, Sic switches to "Flea Fly Flow Fiesta." Sumac has to join in with that one.

Kummaloda Kummaloda Kummalod Vista
Eenie Meenie Desameenie, Ooo Wadda Wadda Meenie . . .

CardaMom's the first adult to crack: "Enough!"

"Eenty teenty figgery fell."

They all turn toward Grumps.

The old man mutters the words more than singing them, staring into space. "Ell dell doman ell, turkey turkey torry rope, am tam toory jock, you are IT!" Pointing at PopCorn. "That's how we'd choose, for Hide and Seek."

"Back in Glasgow, this was?" asks MaxiMum.

"Load of tosh," says Grumps, instead of answering, and his face is all closed again.

Sic's phone plays something ironic. "Oh, hey, Jag, thanks

for getting back to me! Just hanging, yeah . . ." He wanders away from the group.

"If that *Jag* was PapaDum's brother Jagroop," says MaxiMum loudly, "you should call him Taya, just like you call his younger brother Chacha."

"Why do Hindi family words have to be so complicated?" complains Catalpa.

"Family is complicated," PopCorn tells her with a grin. "English just obscures that fact by using so few words for it."

CardaMom says goodbye to the homeless guy and turns back to the family with a "Come on," as if it wasn't her keeping them waiting. "Sic can catch us up."

"I'll wait out here," says Grumps when they reach the sign that says Toytally Awesome.

"Have you ever even been in a toy shop, Dad?" PopCorn asks him.

"Not that I recall."

"Yeah, *I* recall a lot of playing with stones."

"Stimulated your imagination, didn't it?" says Grumps.

"Then let's walk around the block to stretch our legs, Iain," MaxiMum suggests.

"My legs are long enough." He takes up his position against the wall.

Sic canters up to them.

"No luck with Taya?" asks Catalpa, reading his face.

"Are you planning to phone up everyone you're related to in the Greater Toronto Area and pester them into teaching you to drive?"

"Everyone he knows," MaxiMum corrects her. "I heard him earlier giving the spiel to his old tennis teacher."

"Your big brother's a dog with a bone," PopCorn tells Oak, planting kisses all over that sweat-sticky baby head.

"This reminds me of a Whac-A-Mole game," sighs Sic, "with all of you dashing my hopes, *bam, bam.*"

"Why don't you figure out something you can trade for lessons," suggests CardaMom, "so you're not being a parasite?"

"What a *parasite?*" asks Brian.

"When you jump out of an airplane, it stops you smashing to death," Aspen tells her.

The Lotterys can't help laughing even though Brian's looking distinctly alarmed.

"That's a *parachute,*" says MaxiMum, "and none of you are to jump out of any airplanes —"

"Not till my eighteenth birthday," puts in Sic with a grin.

"A parasite is a user, someone who's all take and no give," says CardaMom. "Like a bloodsucker, or a tapeworm living in your gut."

"Great, now you'll really give Brian nightmares," says

PopCorn. "We were better off with the jumping out of airplanes."

"Park your fire truck outside the store now," Sumac reminds Brian.

"You guard it?" Brian asks Grumps.

He doesn't say no.

Brian lifts it off — luckily she's got an undershirt on — and places it beside him warily.

Oak comes in with them, but he's easy to distract. If he seems to be enjoying a toy, one of them says, "Hey, Oak, Oaky-doke, look at this one," and lifts him away while someone else smuggles the first thing to the cash register.

"Nothing made of wood, moppets," PopCorn pleads. (Because last year Dadi Ji and Dada Ji gave Oak a set of antique-looking alphabet blocks and he threw one of them and it split Catalpa's lip open.)

"Does bamboo count as wood?" asks Sumac.

"Well, it's pretty light, as wood goes," says CardaMom.

Sic reads the handwritten label hanging by a ribbon: *"Sustainably sourced shakers with lovingly knitted organic covers."*

PopCorn's crouched over a puppet theater, letting out cooing sounds. Sumac is tempted to shush him, but he's in such a state of bliss. . . .

"A set of cardboard prisms, pyramids, and dodecahedrons?" she suggests.

227

"Oak will suck them and make them gooey," Aspen objects, very sensibly for her.

Sumac knew that, really; she just wanted them for herself.

"Forty-nine dollars ninety-five cents for a bib?" says Catalpa. "Suckers!"

"It's ancient-grain hemp, ultra thirsty, hand edged," says the woman behind the counter.

CardaMom gives Catalpa a *mind your manners* look.

Sumac wonders how a bib can be thirsty.

Aspen's riding way too fast on the Cuddly Rocking Hippo and almost knocks over an Eiffel Tower made of Legos, so Sic sends her outside.

Catalpa checks her phone again. "Yarn-bombing with Quinn's on again! See ya."

"Be back before dinner," says CardaMom.

"Probably."

"Better be," says Sic, "since you're making Moroccan apricot stew."

Catalpa groans. "The one with the carrots *and* the sweet potatoes *and* the squash *and* the eggplant *and* the peppers *and* the zucchini?"

"Good recall! I'll help with the cutting up," says CardaMom.

"When do we get to meet this new inseparable friend Quinn?" asks PopCorn.

Catalpa flicks her hair out of her face scornfully.

"Can we hear a track from Game of Moans, at least?" asks Sic.

"Tones!"

Sumac and Aspen share a grin.

"You're so easy to get a rise out of," Sic says to Catalpa's departing back, "it's not even satisfying."

PopCorn's up on a Brachiosaurus Fold-out Step Set now, trying to reach the last Samurai Finger Puppet on the top shelf.

"How much?" Brian asks, holding up a net of marbles.

Sumac glances at the handwritten tag. "Only four ninety-five, but Oak's too young for those; he'll try to eat them."

"Not for Oaky-doke."

"That's right."

"I gots four ninety-five in piggy?"

"You probably do, *tsi't-ha*," says CardaMom, "but we're not going to buy marbles."

"I buy them my money out my piggy," Brian tells her.

"Not today, honeychild."

Just then PopCorn gets the nosepiece of his glasses

entangled in the invisible thread of a mobile of the solar system. "We can't take you anywhere," Sumac hisses, smacking his butt, but not hard.

Finally the Lotterys have picked a few good presents for Oak. "We don't take the tags off till we've paid for them," Sic reminds Aspen, scooping a set of beanbags out of her hands.

Like playing tag, Sumac thinks: A *tag* means you can't get away.

"Mission accomplished, and we didn't even break anything," whoops PopCorn, carrying Oak out of the shop upside down, frog shoes waving in the air.

Outside, MaxiMum's buying a magazine from a woman with one cloudy eye and listening to her views on the mayor, while Aspen's practicing handstands against the window of a bank. Grumps is finishing a cigarette and staring in the opposite direction.

Sumac helps Brian fit her truck on over her head and put the strings back on the red marks on her shoulders. "Don't they hurt?"

"Nope," lies Brian.

Sumac walks beside Grumps, trying to think of something off-putting to mention about this neighborhood. Unfortunately they pass three swanky stores in a row: artisanal cheese, custom-designed cakes, and one-of-a-kind chairs. Nothing to off-put him here. "Oodles of graffiti, aren't there?" she says, pointing.

No answer from her grandfather.

"Catalpa's gone off to do it with wool."

Grumps's forehead creases as if he has no idea what she means.

"Oh, look, there's the rehab center for drug addicts," Sumac says, pointing it out. Two badly sunburned men are half lying on the step: all the better. "And that shop there is a tiny little mosque," she adds. She bets he doesn't like mosques. The bait shop, hm; would Grumps think worms were *weirdy*, or does he like fishing?

He doesn't respond to any of this.

As they pass a Caribbean café, Sumac asks, "Do you like roti?" Hoping he doesn't.

"Roast?"

"No, roti, like potato curry wrapped in bread. Sometimes with goat in it," she adds with relish; she's pretty sure that Grumps doesn't eat goat.

Shouts, from behind them. "Excuse me! Excuse me!"

It's the woman from Toytally Awesome, all out of breath and hair stuck to her face as she catches up with the Lotterys. "I'm sorry, but — your boy stole something." Pointing at Brian.

"She's a girl," says Aspen before anyone can stop her.

"*Not* a girl," objects Brian.

PopCorn and CardaMom exchange a helpless glance.

"Well, he — there's an item in his, in her pocket," says the woman confusedly.

Brian grips the sides of her fire truck as if she's about to speed off in it.

"Maybe you took a toy and forgot to pay, sweet peach?" PopCorn murmurs.

"I gots four ninety-five in piggy but CardaMom say no!" Eyes brimming, Brian reaches down below her fire truck and yanks the marbles out of the pocket of her shorts.

CardaMom sighs. "I'm so sorry, it was a misunderstanding. Brian, can you give them back, please?"

But the tiny hand stays locked.

The woman from Toytally Awesome grabs hold of the net.

"Our Grumps need marbles!" Brian pulls back. One marble, then another, then a whole flood of them cascades to the sidewalk.

Aspen bursts out laughing.

"He's lost his marbles." Sumac's nearly shouting it. "Our grandfather. That's what Brian means, he's got dementia, and she thinks —"

Grumps narrows his eyes at Sumac as if she's the rudest person in the world.

Her whole head goes hot.

Aspen chases in all directions, picking up fistfuls of marbles and making a bag of her T-shirt to hold them.

The woman from the store is looking appalled.

"I finded just one in the playground only small," sobs Brian, tears scudding down her face.

"Losing your marbles, that just means you can't think too clearly," MaxiMum is saying to Brian very quietly.

"That why I tookeded them! There be big boss ones so Grumps can think extra well —" Then Brian remembers the ripped bag is empty and shakes it tragically.

"Gotcha," Aspen says. She's facedown in the gutter, snatching a handful from the brink of a storm drain.

"What do we owe you?" PopCorn asks the store owner.

She flaps her hands. "That's all right."

"No, no, ma'am, you're very kind, but . . ." He hurries back toward Toytally Awesome at her side.

MaxiMum lets out one of her long meditation breaths. "Right. Every last marble off this street before someone falls over one and breaks a hip."

The Lotterys collect them all, or nearly.

"Did you know the more you cry the less you have to pee?" Sumac tells Brian, to cheer her up.

"That interesting," Brian admits, sniffling.

She goes over to Grumps with one huge marble.

He looks at it as if it's a dog poop and turns away.

I hate him, thinks Sumac. Relieved to let herself say it, even if it's only in the privacy of her own head.

Aspen insists on tying a knot in her T-shirt to hold the marbles in, jogging home with her tummy and ribs showing below a bobbing attachment like some kind of tumor.

Sumac catches up with CardaMom. "I only explained about the dementia so the woman wouldn't think Brian's a robber," she says in a small voice.

"I know."

"If it's a true thing, why is it a secret?"

"It's not, not exactly. It's a touchy subject," says CardaMom.

PopCorn catches up with the Lotterys.

"What's that?" asks MaxiMum, pointing at his elegant paper bag sealed with a ribbon.

"She wouldn't let me pay for the blasted marbles, kept saying what a 'sweet little person' Brian is, so I had to grab the first thing I saw, which was the fifty-dollar thirsty bib."

Sumac almost laughs, but swallows it so her throat hurts.

✳

On Thursday it's even hotter. Aspen comes down to dinner stark naked. When CardaMom tells her to put some clothes on, Aspen says, "FYI, your Mohawk ancestors — the kids traditionally didn't wear anything in the summer." With a glance at their grandfather to see if he's shocked.

"Well, this is a nontraditional household, so you can wear my apron," says CardaMom, slipping it over Aspen's head before she can object. It's the huge sparkly one that says *That's Opportunity Knocking, So Don't Complain About the Noise!* and it comes down nearly to Aspen's ankles.

Disappointingly, Grumps is ignoring the whole thing; he's tucking into PapaDum's twelve-layer lasagna as if he's starving. Sumac supposes Italian doesn't count as what he calls *ethnic food*.

She hardly eats any lasagna herself because she's nervous about her presentation.

"Scored a driving coach, by the way," announces Sic, very blasé.

"Seriously?" asks Catalpa. "You've guilted or tricked some adult into —"

"I have entered into a mutually beneficial arrangement with a local entrepreneur," he interrupts, "which incidentally is going to look fantastic on my résumé. In exchange for a complete overhaul of her antiquated website, Mrs. Zhao will be putting me on her insurance as an Occasional Driver and taking me out three evenings a week."

Amazement all around. "In the Poop Cube?" asks Sumac.

"The salesman told her it was called Bitter Chocolate Pearl."

"What's all the hoo-ha?" Grumps wants to know.

PapaDum explains.

"Driving, that's useful, anyway," says the old man.

High praise, indeed: Sic waggles his eyebrows at Sumac. "Our gracious neighbor's a tough negotiator," he adds. "I argued that web design of my caliber is a way more specialist skill than driving, but she pointed out that I need this deal at least twice as much as she does . . . so I have to do two hours' work for every hour she takes me on the road."

"We should go talk to her," says CardaMom to the other parents, "check she's not just being nice."

PopCorn snorts. "Nice? This is Mrs. Zhao we're talking about."

"Well, it proves that anything's possible," says PapaDum.

"Or maybe that there's nothing Sic can study that'll get him farther than his powers of persuasion," says CardaMom.

"Never needed to study charm, Momma," he says with a Southern accent and a smirk.

It occurs to Sumac that this is the ideal moment, because everyone seems to be in a relatively good mood. "Can I do a presentation?"

"Sure," says PapaDum. "More Mesopotamians?"

"Actually —"

"Is this going to take long?" Catalpa's on her feet already. "Because Sheryl and Celize and Quinn and I —"

"Your friends can wait ten minutes," says CardaMom, nudging Catalpa back into her chair with one finger.

"Are we still on for a starlight hike tonight?" Wood asks PapaDum.

He nods, finger to lips, and gestures to Sumac.

"This week I've been — I was curious about homes," Sumac begins a little unevenly, and has to clear her throat.

"Oh, like cross-culturally?" asks PopCorn. "High-rises versus igloos, that sort of thing?"

She hesitates, fiddling with the projector so the first image — a sleek modern building against an orangey evening sky — hits the white wall of the Mess. The last slideshow she did, of the childhood photos, went pear-shaped, but this time she's totally prepared. "It turns out, it just so happens, that there are some really, uh, world-class residential facilities with lots of facilities" — she said that already — "I mean, lots of stuff for people who are . . . not so young anymore." Her gaze touching down on Grumps, who's still working on his second helping of lasagna. "Right here in Toronto," she adds, to prove that the Lotterys could easily visit Grumps. If he wanted them to. "For instance, here's a great example called Sunset Vista Residence, where nurses come in *round the clock*. Only if you need something, obviously, otherwise they don't," she throws in his direction, remembering how much it annoys him even to hear Lotterys talking on the stairs at seven in the morning. She clicks onto the next image, a blue-tiled indoor pool. "You can swim; there's a resistance section where the water actually pushes against your muscles to strengthen them. And here we see the, the *per*gola in the garden." She's not sure she's pronouncing the trellis thing right.

"Sumac," says PapaDum in an odd voice.

"Pergola, sorry," she says, rushing on because she can't stop for questions, she hasn't made any of her really important points yet. "The mission statement of Sunset Vista says, uh, it's about *living your life to the fullest in a homelike environment.* You get whatever help you want, like with . . ." Here she's meant to read from the list that starts *bathing, dressing, eating,* but she falters, because she can't imagine Grumps standing for anyone treating him like a baby. "They offer a *personalized package of assistance,*" Sumac quotes instead — she can't help picturing that as a huge present with a bow on top — "which means you pick your bits, your favorite *amenities,*" she says, dredging up the word from her memory. "Like, you don't have to have the deep tissue aromatherapy massage if you don't like people pawing you." Wasn't that what Grumps called it the other day, *pawing,* when CardaMom offered to rub cream on his sunburned shoulders? "You can play euchre instead, or billiards, or you can sightsee. . . ." Should that be *see sights?*

"*Tsi't-ha,* let me stop you there." That's CardaMom.

Sumac can't find where she is in her notes, but she knows she's got a long way to go, so she mustn't stop or even take a second to say why she's not stopping. Wood's got his hand over his eyes, she notices, and Catalpa's mouth is twisted. Sumac just needs to reach one picture of Sunset Vista that looks so fabulously luxurious, they'll all see what she means. "There's lots of individual privacy and a special *memory care unit* for" — her nerve fails her on *dementia* — "what you, what lots of seniors have got in their heads," she says in Grumps's direction, but not meeting his gaze. It only strikes her now, wouldn't stashing the confused oldies side by side in their own unit make them even more confused? She's flicking through the slides too quickly, and none of these beaming, silver-haired people look anything like Grumps. Nobody's shown with a cigarette; Sumac couldn't find any old folks' home that even mentioned smoking. Without looking at him directly she can see that PopCorn's face is a mask. It's all somehow going wrong, horribly wrong, Sumac knows, but she can't fix it by stopping in the middle, she just has to push on to the end and use all her *powers of persuasion*, just like Sic. "Look, a movie theater with surround sound!" No, that's the chapel. She flicks back two slides, desperate to find the movie theater, but all she can find is a tour bus and a picture of a cake stand.

"Sumac!" PapaDum's voice booms.

She reads aloud the captions on the photos in a gabble. *"Excursions to Niagara Falls. Enhanced retirement living. Come relax with us, because you deserve —"*

Snap: Sic, leaning across the table, has shut the laptop. The wall goes blank.

A screech from Grumps's chair as he shoves it back. He gives Sumac a baleful stare, then turns it on the whole family. "Believe me, ye couldn't long to see the back of me more than I long to see the back of ye!"

He crashes out into the Hall of Mirrors. Then they hear the door of the Grumpery slam behind him.

CardaMom breaks the awful hush: "Sumac, how could you?"

Her voice comes out in a squeak. "I was only trying to help."

"I find that hard to believe," says MaxiMum.

Sumac struggles to keep the tears in her eye sockets.

"Did you not realize how much it would hurt his feelings?" asks PapaDum.

"Yeah," says Catalpa, "how would you feel if we stuck you in some institution just because you're über irritating?"

"I only thought" — Sumac gasps for breath — "if I could find him a home that's almost like a real one, somewhere he'd prefer to live than Camelottery, without all the things that bug him so much, without all of *us* — because he doesn't want to stay here —"

She looks from face to face. None of them can deny that.

"But maybe he wants us to *want* him to stay," says PopCorn in a voice so flat that it doesn't sound like his.

It was cruel, what Sumac did: She can suddenly see that now. How can she have spent all week preparing her presentation and not noticed the mean-mindedness of it? What kind of a blundering idiot is she?

Now her tears spill down, and she flees from the room as if she's three instead of nine.

✳

When various parents come up to the attic to knock at Sumac's door, she shouts, "Go away," and buries her sticky face under the pillow again.

Sic doesn't ask permission, he just walks in. "Poor duck," he says, and sits down on her butt.

Sumac wiggles to shake him off.

"Oh, what a lovely cushion," he says, adjusting his weight. "A little bony, maybe . . . could do with some reupholstering . . . a bit more duck down . . ."

"Reupholster yourself," she says, her voice muffledly.

He bounces up and down.

She groans but doesn't mind, oddly enough. When you're this miserable, having a heavy weight press you flat feels right.

"Seriously, Smackeroo," says her brother. "Have you figured out why everyone got so mad at you?"

Sumac cringes. "I know I know I know, I was stupid and horrible, I don't need to hear it all over again!" She twists sideways till Sic tips off her.

He's shaking his head. "Wouldn't we all heave a massive,

collective sigh of relief if the dude volunteered to move to some spa-type retirement villa?"

She blinks at him.

"What you got in trouble for was saying it out loud."

"Yeah, well, I wish I hadn't."

"You think MaxiMum's enjoying having to talk him into cutting his dinosaurish toenails? Even CardaMom, with her blind spot about family —"

Sumac is confused. "Blind spot like in a car?"

"Right, the bit you can't see clearly: She's all about family. And PapaDum can't stand the guy — probably hopes he'll snuff it in his sleep one of these hot nights."

"You're sick, Sic." She's grinning behind her hand.

He shrugs and fluffs out his Afro. "I've been mulling it over, and the thing of it is, it's . . . payback time!"

Sometimes when her brother talks like one of his video games, Sumac has no idea what he means. "Payback for what?"

"PopCorn had scaly eczema and projectile vomiting till he was two, remember?"

"He's probably exaggerating," says Sumac.

"Well, of course, doesn't he always? But still. If your folks get you to eighteen in one piece, you owe them something," says Sic. "So PopCorn has to be loyal to his dad, and we're loyal to PopCorn: links in a chain."

The kind that keeps a prisoner shackled to a wall, Sumac thinks.

"Anyway, cheer up, fellow mutt. It's all good."

"No it's not," she tells him.

"It's Oak's birthday tomorrow. *Let the wild rumpus start!*" Sic quotes.

"Yeah," says Sumac, but not feeling it.

CHAPTER 11

- - - - - - - - - - - - - - - - - - -

LOSEDED . . . AND FINDED

Sumac remembers Oak's first birthday, when they dressed him up as an acorn in that velvety brown costume with the matching cap and invited everyone from his physiotherapist and his and Brian's caseworker, to all the relations within driving distance, and even the babies from his music games class . . . though Oak did fall asleep over his bottle before most of them arrived.

No party this year. The parents say *things are busy enough at the moment*, which Sumac knows is a euphemism for Grumps. Since her mortifying presentation on old folks' homes yesterday, she's avoided everybody's eyes, but especially his.

She taps on the door of the Asp Pit, which has a picture of a huge snake with Aspen's grinning face.

Aspen's lying on her back in the sea of Legos that flows from wall to wall with her legs hooked over her elbows, talking to some small, complicated flying machine she's making. "What?"

"The plan's on hold for now," whispers Sumac.

"What plan?"

She grunts in exasperation. "The plan to get Grumps to ask to go live somewhere else."

Aspen's face clears and she rocks a little on her spine. "Oh, I wasn't doing that anymore anyway."

"Why not?" asks Sumac.

"Slate likes him."

She frowns at Aspen. "How do you know?"

"Well, I left him in his bed this morning —"

"You left Slate in bed?"

"In Grumps's bed, duh! And I listened outside the door, I thought it would be hilarious, but actually Grumps just said, *Who have we here?* and when I looked in a few minutes later he was tickling Slate's tummy, and I had to do a big fake like, *Oo, is that where you got to?*"

Sumac grits her teeth. That rat is such a sucker for tickles.

So she's totally alone, she realizes as she stomps downstairs. Despite what Sic told her last night about how everybody would prefer it if Grumps left voluntarily, Sumac is clearly the only one who's having trouble putting up with him. She always thought she was pretty kind and tolerant, but it turns out she's the sourpuss of the family. Not Fragrant but Poison Sumac.

It's him, she sobs in her head. *Grumps made me like this. It's him and not me.*

This afternoon the Lotterys take the Birthday-in-a-Bag picture of Oak, a custom that began because Sic looked so comical when the midwives weighed him in a cloth sling dangling from a scale the day he was born. (It's harder to do with the adult birthdays, but the Lotterys manage, using a sleeping bag.) Then they stand Oak up against the back of the Shed and paint his silhouette around last year's smaller one. (Sumac usually loves looking at all nine of her different colored outlines, but not today. Growing up just means you make bigger mistakes and get into worse trouble.)

Next, each of the Lotterys writes Oak a letter about what they love about him — *evRyTing,* insists Brian's short note — and they put them in a big envelope in his file. Then they take him by his plumpy creased wrists and ankles to give him the bumps, very slowly wheeing him up toward the sky and down to the ground, twice for age two and another one for luck.

"Do me," begs Aspen, "do me, really fast and high!"

"Only on your birthday," says Sic.

"Please!"

"Otherwise they wouldn't be the birthday bumps, would they?"

After dinner, they wait for MaxiMum to get back from her walk. (Sometimes she has to be alone so her head won't pop.) PapaDum and PopCorn struggle with the melting icing on the snowman cake, while the others go upstairs to scatter balloons all across the Loud Lounge and let Oak crawl around, biffing them into the air.

Catalpa's trying out some tricky fingering on her guitar while Wood buries himself in something called the *SAS Survival Handbook*. Aspen's cat's cradling at top speed, trying to teach Brian a way too complicated figure called Cheating the Hangman. Grumps slurps his tea. Sumac reads a graphic novel called *Cardboard* that she found gripping last time, but she keeps losing her place.

"I bet it's nearly time to light your two candles," murmurs CardaMom, scooping up Oak.

"Shouldn't the *c-a-k-e* be a surprise for him?" asks Catalpa.

"Oh, but he'll love watching the candles get lit, the whole procedure. . . . We'll call you all down to the Mess when it's ready."

"Two?" says Grumps when CardaMom and Oak are gone. "Why two candles?"

"Oak be two," says Brian.

He frowns at her. "That wee fellow can't be more than one."

"My baby brother two today."

"You're getting your numbers mixed up, girlie."

"*Not* a girlie," shrieks Brian.

Sumac intervenes. "Oak's just not very big yet because he didn't grow much before he came to live with us."

"But the child can barely stand up."

Her blood starts to boil.

"Yeah, Oak's slow," says Wood coldly. "So?"

"Needs to build up his legs," says the old man. "Wouldn't he get around faster in one of those walker things?"

"No, but he's *slow*," says Aspen.

"As in, delayed," says Catalpa. "Somebody shook him when he was tiny, before we got him."

That's the part of her little brother's story Sumac tries to keep filed away at the very back of her mind. The idea of an adult who was meant to be looking after a baby rattling him hard enough to bruise his brain — "Weren't you told?"

Wood says what they're all thinking: "Maybe it slipped your mind?"

"There was some talk of a problem," snaps Grumps, "but I didn't think it was the baby was meant, that's all."

Now Sumac's furious. *You're the one who's a problem*, she wants to shout. Oak has problems but he's not a problem, he's 100 percent wonderful, whereas this old man is one big stinky problem.

Catalpa stalks onto the landing and shouts down through the house. "Is it time for the cake yet?"

"Just a few last-minute repairs," CardaMom calls back up from the Mess. "Play a game or something!"

They stare at each other across the carpeted expanse of the Loud Lounge.

"Tickle fight?" suggests Aspen.

Sumac shakes her head at her. Monopoly? No, she decides, that always leads to war.

"You know Napoleon games?" Brian asks Grumps.

"What's that?" he says.

"Games from the old days, she means," says Catalpa. "Like, Napoleonic times."

And if Grumps says he isn't from Napoleonic times,

Sumac's going to tell him that she wishes he was, so he'd be long buried by now.

"All sorts of games, we had," Grumps says instead. "There was none of this *screen time* nonsense."

"I wish I could live inside a screen, like Vanellope the Glitch," says Aspen.

"What gameses?" Brian asks Grumps.

He shrugs. "Don't remember off the top of my head. Cards, clapping things, skipping —"

"I know to skip!"

But Sumac's appalled at the prospect of Grumps trying to skip. "We don't have a rope up here."

"Catalpa," CardaMom calls from downstairs, "could you take Oak for a few minutes?"

Catalpa sighs and goes out.

Another longer silence. "Blind Man's Buff," says Grumps.

"Cool!" Aspen leaps up.

Well, if their grandfather's willing to play a game with them, Sumac supposes they should go along with it, though it's not going to be any fun.

Wood's phone laughs hollowly in his pocket. "One sec." He steps out of the Loud Lounge.

"Do you play it so when you're tagged you're It, or you're out?" asks Sumac. She wants to get the rules straight so nobody will accuse her of being a *cheetah*.

The old man shrugs. "Suit yourself."

"But what's the rule, do you remember?" Sumac waits. "Will I look it up?" She wishes Wood would finish his call and come back and help.

"It doesn't matter a — either way," says Grumps, sounding so cranky that Sumac decides they'd better get on with it.

"We'll go visit my Turret, will we?" That's Catalpa talking to Oak on the landing.

For a blindfold, Sumac improvises with Brian's bandana. Brian wants to be It, but then gets nervous and pulls the bandana off. So Sumac blindfolds herself scrupulously till she can't see a thing.

"No chasing," squeals Brian. There's a thump, as if she's backed into something.

"But, Brian," says Aspen, "it's a chasing game. Like Tag."

"Do game but no chasing me."

Sumac stretches out her hands and moves off, making sure to avoid the area where Brian's squeaks are coming from. But she doesn't want to touch Grumps either. So she steps cautiously, fingering her way around beanbags and chairs.

"You'd catch a fellow and feel his face," says Grumps, "till you could make a stab at who he was."

Sumac feels sick at the thought of stroking the old man's bristly face, or having his fingers on hers.

"I'm bored," she hears Aspen say, on the way out onto the landing.

"Come back," Sumac pleads. "Aspen! You can be It if you like —"

She bumps into Brian, who peeps in delight.

Sumac pulls off the blindfold with relief.

"Not me. Grumps be It," Brian insists.

Sumac fixes the blindfold on him, nervous-fingered.

"Not too tight," he barks.

So she loosens the bandana. Now it's sliding down his nose.

"I'll do it myself." He pushes her hands out of the way.

"I'm sick of waiting," Aspen's complaining to Catalpa next door in the Turret. "I don't even eat cake."

"Then what do you care how long it takes?" asks Catalpa.

Grumps makes the blindfold even tighter than Sumac did the first time, so the hem digs into his cheeks and flattens his ears. He edges around the room. Sumac ducks in to pull a chair out of his way so he won't fall over it.

"Yoo-hoo," Brian calls, taunting him.

Aspen must have left the door of the Turret open, because Oak crawls into the Loud Lounge now, gurgling wetly.

"We playing Blind Man's Buff," Brian calls out to him.

Sumac tiptoes up close to Grumps, touches him with one finger on his back, then runs. Then Grumps nearly catches Brian because she's doubled over laughing, so Sumac has to yank her out of the way by her tank top.

"Impossible! The room's too big, I'll never find ye," says Grumps. As he bends over, pawing the air, his cigarette pack falls out of his shirt pocket.

"Ew," says Brian, picking it up.

"Where are my ciggies?" he demands.

"Dirty," says Brian. "Put in the trash."

"No you don't, you little —"

"They kills you," says Brian.

"I'll kill you if you don't give back my property!" He lurches in the direction of her voice with his arms out stiffly.

Oak thinks this is some kind of wonderful game. He's crawling toward Grumps as —

The big hard boot comes down on his hand.

Their little brother doesn't make a sound, at first. That's how Sumac knows it's bad. Oak's mouth opens in a stunned O.

"You stood on him," she shrieks.

Grumps stumbles backward and yanks the bandana off his red face.

And then such a howl goes up from Oak, and Sumac is scooping him up, and running down and down and down through the house, wrestling with each baby gate and leaving it swinging open, because this is an emergency and she can't be sensible, can't be a *rational being*, she's crying even louder than Oak, trying to make herself heard: "He stood on him!"

CardaMom in the Mess, a smear of icing on her eyebrow: "Calm down. Who? What?"

Grumps seems too cozy a name for the intruder. "Your father," Sumac screams at PopCorn. "He stamped on Oak's hand!"

PopCorn stares back at her.

PapaDum has a bag of frozen edamame wrapped in a napkin in a couple of seconds, and presses it on Oak's tiny fingers.

The front door — MaxiMum coming home. Sumac runs to tell her too.

MaxiMum listens without a word, then goes up the stairs two at a time and intercepts Grumps on the Treadmill Landing. "Iain!" For once, her voice isn't calm and level. "What happened?"

"Ah, ah, I suppose you'd call it a wee kerfuffle," he says. "Collision? Is that what I mean?"

"Wee?" repeats MaxiMum.

Grumps pushes past her and comes down the stairs. In the Mess, he's breathless and shaking, Sumac notices, the bandana still around his neck as if he's dressed up as a cowboy. "I hope he's not hurt?"

PopCorn steps up very close to him. "Dad, did you stand on Oak's hand?"

"Well, I'm sorry, but how was I meant to know he'd got underfoot? Here, give me a look at the poor wee —"

"Get away from me brother!" Brian howls, and keeps howling till Grumps has stepped right back.

"He was mad at us." The words spill out of Sumac. "He told Brian he was going to kill her because she took his cigarettes, and then he chased us and —" If she tries hard enough she can even hear it in her memory: the tiny crunch when the giant sole came down on Oak's soft fingers.

"OK," says PapaDum, making a gesture for Sumac to stop talking now.

"It wasn't — that's not the way it was at all, at all," says Grumps. "Didn't see the little bugger, did I?"

"Enough!" says PapaDum in a grizzly-bear voice Sumac has never heard him use before.

✳

The doctor at Emergency remembered them from previous visits due to *aspendents*. Aspen was very smug that it wasn't her who got hurt (or hurt anyone else) this time. Oak doesn't have a cast; the broken finger's just buddy-taped to the next one, which means the two of them have to be buddies for a couple of weeks and do all their moving together till the tiny crack heals.

Last night Sumac must have dozed off a few times, but mostly she was wide-awake, staring at the slanted ceiling of the attic that's pretending to be hers. This morning she's nauseous.

The doctor said to put an ice pack on the finger for twenty minutes out of every hour, but Oak doesn't like that. Also, the Lotterys are meant to keep checking to see if it's cold or blue, which is hard to tell because anything you put ice on gets cold. They comfort Oak by giving him a lollipop and putting him in the bath, but the hurt hand has to be kept dry in a plastic bag taped at the wrist, and Oak thinks this is hilarious and keeps punching the water to make tsunamis.

"At least your finger's not pointing sideways," Aspen tells him.

"Ghah," he says, grinning back at her.

"Yeah, not bent like a paper clip," adds Wood.

"With shards of bone coming through the skin," says Aspen.

"Shut up!" Sumac tells them. How can they be cracking jokes at a time like this?

Grumps hasn't emerged from his room today. Sumac hasn't even heard any angry toilet flushing. He hasn't had any breakfast or lunch, which is fine by Sumac; he deserves to starve.

The quote in neat print on the mirror in the hall is almost definitely MaxiMum's:

suffering is inevitable,
misery is optional.

Sumac puzzles over it for a minute before she decides that it's Buddhist for *suck it up*. Well, Grumps can suck it up: All the family he's got left hate him, and he has nobody to blame but himself.

Around four, PapaDum brings out Oak's birthday cake that never got eaten yesterday. MaxiMum zooms Oak near enough to blow out his two candles (with discreet help from Aspen at the side) but yanks him back before he can grab the flames.

Sumac just picks at her slice.

"Not hungry, whippersnapper?" asks PopCorn.

"It's too sticky."

"The cake?"

"The day."

She tries to have a nap, but the coolness of the air conditioning doesn't reach the attic, because hot air rises. In her old room, she'd have been pleasantly chilly, but Grumps is in there, with the door shut, probably puffing away on two cigarettes at once and not caring about the *little bugger* he trod on.

Sumac rolls over, searching for a less scorching bit of the pillow.

Awkward fact: Grumps didn't step on Oak on purpose.

Yeah, but it wasn't pure accident either, was it?

He was blindfolded; he didn't know Oak was there. That's the bit Sumac failed to mention last night.

Yeah, but Grumps would have known Oak was *under-foot* if he'd been paying attention, because Brian called out to Oak when he crawled into the Loud Lounge. So it was negligence plus carelessness and bad temper.

Hang on, did Brian actually say Oak's name?

Sumac can't remember. She's a bad noticer.

Probably somebody else has mentioned the blindfold to the moms and dads by now: Aspen, or Brian, or Grumps himself. It shouldn't be always up to Sumac to report every little detail.

He was definitely mad with Brian about the cigarettes, anyway.

Yeah, but he wasn't mad with Oak, was he?

Well, losing your temper makes you clumsy, so Grumps might have stepped on Oak even if he hadn't been blind-folded. And he definitely didn't care enough. He called it a *wee collision* and didn't say sorry! Or — Sumac tries to remember — maybe he said a quick sorry, but you could tell he hardly meant it.

The way she told it last night may not have been true in every tiny detail, but it was true in spirit, because Grumps probably does long to stomp on all the Lotterys. He's a par-asite, all take and no give.

Argh. Sumac's got to get out of this not-her-room. As she goes downstairs, past the door of Catalpa's Turret, she hears Oak doing his usual babble. She puts her head in —

And finds Oak playing with three hairbrushes while Catalpa's kissing some boy. Wet smoochy kissing so Sumac can hardly even see the boy's face.

"Get *out*," Catalpa screeches.

"Sorry, I am, I am."

As Sumac shuts the door behind her fast, a wail goes up from Oak.

She considers telling the nearest parent that Catalpa is not exactly concentrating on elevating Oak's finger. Then decides to keep her big mouth shut, for once.

She follows the smell of warm pie down to the Mess. Sic is there, sipping ginger iced tea.

"But why did Mrs. Zhao take you through a major intersection on day one?" CardaMom is demanding.

"She knows no fear. She's used to Beijing traffic," Sic says shakily. "When she shouts, I can't understand her accent, but I don't want to say so in case she gets even madder. . . ."

"Maybe she's not so much bossy as Confucian," says PapaDum.

"Confusing?" asks Aspen, upside down against the refrigerator, where she's practicing a headstand.

"Confucianism, the ancient Chinese philosophy," CardaMom tells her. "The young should respect their elders and all that."

"Elder doesn't always mean wiser," says Wood.

They're all thinking about Grumps, Sumac can tell.

Catalpa comes down with Oak riding on her hip and the kissing boy behind her. He's pale and skinny, and dressed all in black like her, with quite an interesting face now Sumac can see it.

"Quinn," says PapaDum, "will you stay for some peach pie?"

Ah, so Quinn the crochet-tagger from Game of Tones is not a girl!

He twitchy-smiles and shakes his head instead of answering. Sometimes the Lotterys have that effect on visitors: speechlessness.

"He's got to go," says Catalpa firmly.

On the way out, Quinn gives Oak a little high five — on the hand that's OK.

"I don't know, has he taken any of his meds?" CardaMom mutters to PapaDum.

Grumps again: Nobody needs to say his name.

"Can I bring him a slice of pie?" asks Sic.

"Sure, let's try that. The kettle's boiled," CardaMom tells him.

"Strong, with milk and two sugars," PapaDum adds.

"Talk about rewarding a tantrum!" Sumac didn't mean to say that out loud.

They all turn to look at her.

Under her breath: "He stomps on Oak, and he gets pie?"

"Sumac," says PapaDum, "your grandfather hasn't had anything to eat since yesterday, and hunger makes people irritable. He'll be more prepared for a serious conversation after he's gotten his blood sugar up."

"He's got a tin of toffees under his bed," says Aspen, standing on one leg and leaning over to make a letter *T*.

PapaDum's eyebrows go up. "And what were you doing under his bed?"

"Just looking for something. . . ."

"Yeah, like toffee," says Wood.

"Time for ice," says CardaMom. She approaches Oak with the soft blue ice pack, but he crawls away under the table. "OK, your views are clear," she sighs.

"Listen, kids," says PopCorn, "what happened last night was our fault."

"The fault of us parents, he means," says CardaMom. "Responsibility's a hammock."

"Huh?" says Aspen, upside down in a handstand again.

"It's nice that it's flexible, that we can take turns being in charge," she explains, "but if the hammock stretches too far and somebody falls through . . ."

"Should have stayed in the Loud Lounge while I was on the phone," says Wood gruffly.

"No, it was me," wails Catalpa. "I should have seen Oak crawling out of my room. I just turned my back for a minute to show Aspen a crochet website. . . ."

"One of us big people should have been there too," says MaxiMum. "Iain's eyesight is pretty good, but chasing games can be dangerous."

So nobody's thought to tell them about the blindfold. This would be the moment for Sumac to do that. She opens her mouth to speak —

Nothing comes out.

PopCorn hands Sumac a fragrant, oozing slice on a plate.

Sometimes love *is* a pie. There just isn't enough to go around. Or OK, maybe there is enough love, but not enough time and attention, so you have to grab your piece, and then the pie smashes and you're fighting for crumbs. . . .

What if Sumac had a tiny family? Maybe two parents, one sibling. Or what if she was an only, like Isabella. Something neat and simple.

She closes her eyes. Wishes she could drift away to the ancient land of Sumer.

And then Sic comes galloping back into the Mess, gasping, "He's gone."

*

They check all thirty-two of Camelottery's rooms to find where Grumps might have hidden himself. All the bikes are still in the cage out front. The Wild, the Tree Fort . . . No sign of him. Wood takes Diamond off to search the Ravine.

Sumac's looking in all the closets and spaces big enough for a person to curl up in. When she throws open the linen cupboard, startling Quartz, they both let out a yowl of fright before the cat shoots down from her bed of towels and out the door.

In the Grumpery, the animal heads on the wall stare down at Sumac.

She can hear MaxiMum in the Hall of Mirrors making two search parties of teens and adults to go off down the street in each direction, asking at doors.

The old man's handful of droopy clothes is hanging up in his closet. Ashtray empty. Nothing looks any different.

Maybe Grumps has gone to jump off a bridge, because that would be better than living here.

Pink flowers on the August page. When a monarch butterfly needs a milkweed bush, that's what she heads for, because no other plant will do.

"The airport!" Sumac shrieks. She runs out into the Hall of Mirrors and bumps right into PopCorn. "He's going to fly back to Faro."

He stares at her. Then turns and shouts, "The airport!"

Confusion, consultation, calling a taxi. PopCorn's going because he's his son. And MaxiMum, because Grumps seems to dislike her the least. Sic and Catalpa, long-legged teens for running around the terminal. "I've got super-long legs too," says Aspen, waving one and then the other.

"I can run faster than Catalpa any day," says Wood.

"I'm going too," insists Sumac, surprising herself.

"There won't be room," PapaDum tells her.

"I don't take up much."

"I can't stay here, not knowing," says CardaMom, Oak bouncing in her arms.

"Oh, let's all go," says PapaDum, grabbing PopCorn's phone and hitting redial. "Hi, we just booked a cab. . . . Could you make that two vans?"

Sumac piles into the taxi with the moms (after a brief tussle with Brian, who wants to keep her fire truck on, especially as this is an emergency). They peer out the windows, in case Grumps didn't have enough cash for his own fare and got dropped off a few blocks away. (Or in case I'm wrong, Sumac thinks wildly: What if I'm leading us all in the totally opposite direction from the bridge he's jumping off?)

Once they're on the highway, there are no pedestrians, but Sumac stares at the verges anyway, looking for a tall bearded man stomping along in his work boots. The ride to the airport takes less than half an hour by the clock in the dashboard, but it seems to last forever.

Terminal 1 is an elegant glass eye. The cab slows, passing the Inuksuit stone giants on guard outside Departures. The Lotterys spill out and thump up the escalator.

Under the curved ceiling of Level 3, the check-in hall is vast, full of people. Even if Sumac's right, how will they ever find their grandfather?

"OK," says MaxiMum, pressing Sumac, Aspen, and Wood into a tight cluster, "you're base camp. I'll ask at the ticket counters, and CardaMom will check the washrooms and café."

"You're not allowed in the men's," Wood reminds CardaMom, and races off.

Aspen leaps up and down on the spot.

"Could you stop making a baboon of yourself for one minute?" asks Sumac.

"I'm trying to spot Grumps over the crowd," Aspen tells her.

Racing toddlers, mothers and grandmothers in saris, Orthodox Jewish men with their hats and dangly ringlets, Mennonites in prayer caps and long dresses. . . . Sumac stands staring in all directions, feeling utterly useless. No, worse than that.

"Do you think there's like a Lost Person area?" wonders Aspen.

"He's not lost," snaps Sumac. "He just wants to go home."

Come back! She wails it in her head.

Last night, she should have said loud and clear that Grumps stepping on Oak's finger was a total accident. The kind of thing that happens in a big chaotic house all the time; the kind of thing that's nobody's fault.

But *this* is Sumac's fault: Grumps running off. He's had so much to put up with. Getting his eyebrows burned off, being yanked away from his own life and plonked down in the middle of an unrecognizable one. The unflushed pee, crippled pets, strange vegetables, doors banging, kids underfoot, everybody talking at the same time in smart-ass ways about things he's never heard of. Losing his marbles and being humiliated and poison ivied. Grumps put up with all that, with everything, until Poison Sumac, plotting to stick him in a so-called home, told the whole family that he was a brute who deliberately stomped on their little boy's finger. . . .

She's sweating with panic, despite the chill of the airport.

Grumps is probably feeling just as awful, for different reasons. Guilty about Oak, and miserable about everything, and stressed out by these hordes of people. Right now he'd be trying to get away from everybody and find some room to breathe.

There's a long plate-glass wall over there. Sumac can see the city skyline, gray against pink, and the red lights coming on to mark the Big-Mac-speared-on-an-umbrella silhouette of the CN Tower. Such an alien sight for a small-town man like Grumps.

There? Right by the window, beside a white pillar, where there's a bit of space. Just a sleeve visible behind a cart with five massive suitcases stacked on it.

Sumac takes a step to the left, craning. She almost doesn't want it to be him.

That's Grumps's balding head leaning against the glass. Knobbled fingers locked together, as if he's worn out, or waiting. Not the best of grandfathers. Not even an averagely good one. Not the one any of the Lotterys would have chosen, or he them. But he's theirs.

Aspen's made binoculars of her hands, and she's humming the *Mission: Impossible* theme, so she doesn't even notice Sumac going.

She walks over very slowly. "Hi, Grumps."

The old man blinks, startles. She sees his mouth struggle. "Sue. Sue?"

"Sumac, the tree. But people sometimes hear it as Sue — like, Sue MacClottery," she adds, just to keep the conversation going. Sumac always imagines Sue as a regular girl, an all-rounder, wonderfully average.

"Knew some McLaughterys back in Glasgow."

That surprises her. "It's a real surname?"

"McLaughtery? Of course. A sight realer than Lottery, let me tell you."

That almost makes Sumac smile. "How do you spell it?"

"Like *laughter*, but it rhymes with *otter*. If you ever go to Scotland," says Grumps, "you could introduce yourself as Sue McLaughtery."

She'll travel to Scotland some day, Sumac decides, then go south to England and have more laughs with her cousin Seren. She'll go right around the world on her own, and she won't be just one of the Lotterys, she'll be Sumac Lottery. (Or even Sue McLaughtery, if she prefers.)

A plane takes off, heading west. Grumps's eyes follow it. "They canceled my blasted credit card," he says, as if to himself.

Sumac thinks about all the special powers you get when you turn into an adult: credit cards and driver's licenses and stuff. She never knew they could get taken away again when you're old. "Were you trying to go back to Faro?"

A nod. "My wee house. My car. Still got my driver's license." He pats his back pocket. Then scowls. "Unless they've canceled that too."

"They just want you to be —" Safe? Well? Happy? Sumac doesn't know what to say. "We want you to stay."

His dribbly eyes fix on her.

Only now does she register the shouting in the background. "Sumac!" "Sumac!" Her family must think she's lost too now. "We all came to find you," she tells Grumps.

"What, the whole lot of ye?"

"Sumac!"

She turns around and waves until they see her.

CHAPTER 12

TAGS

All the way home in the van — the one Grumps isn't in — Sumac says nothing. She's so tired, she's dizzy. Instead of dinner, it's buttered toast all round. White bread, even; PapaDum must have bought it specially for Grumps.

After Oak is asleep — and Brian has refused to go to bed or even get into pajamas, despite the fact that Sumac's read her *Room on the Broom* three times — there's a Fleeting at the Trampoline. (Well away from the house, so Grumps won't hear them, Sumac guesses.)

Brian's lying on her back in her fire truck in the middle, waving her arms and legs, a stranded beetle. Aspen is moonwalking around the trampoline to try to flip Brian the right way up.

"Yesterday we called Sunset Vista Residence," MaxiMum begins.

Sumac flinches. The one she showed in her awful presentation? The one her family gave her such grief about?

"The one with the movie theater?" asks Catalpa.

Sic groans.

"We're going to bring Iain there for a visit tomorrow to see how he likes it," says MaxiMum.

He won't. Sumac's sure of that suddenly.

"He doesn't want to watch movies," says Wood between his teeth. "Can't you guys punish him some other way?"

"It's not a punishment," says PapaDum.

Grumps will hate Sunset Vista, even more than he hates Camelottery, Sumac decides. He'll call the resistance pool *unnatural*; he'd rather swim in the lake, and the *round-the-clock* nurses won't let him. He'll refuse to play billiards or

euchre with other random oldies, or go sightseeing. He probably won't be allowed to smoke even in the pergolas in the garden. Nobody there will give a hoot about him because they don't know Iain Miller; he's nobody to them.

"It's about making sure your grandfather gets the care he needs," says MaxiMum.

"Yeah, right," says Sic.

Aspen bounces wordlessly, for once, watching faces. Brian yawns, watching the stars. The monitor on MaxiMum's belt transmits Oak's small dreaming murmurs.

"Attacking Oak, then running off . . . Iain's dementia's clearly getting worse fast," says PapaDum.

Sumac can't speak: It's as if her throat's been filled up with cement.

A tear runs down CardaMom's nose, and MaxiMum slides an arm around her. "Maybe we were naive," CardaMom sobs. "Bit off a lot more than we could chew." Almost laughing: "This is what comes of being the family that likes to say why not."

PopCorn speaks up hoarsely. "My bad. My dad. My big dumb idea in the first place."

"It was worth a try," PapaDum tells him.

"Experiments always are," says MaxiMum.

"No!" Sumac blinks the tears away. "Listen. There's something — I — I — I —"

"Take a breath, *beta*," says PapaDum.

What Sic said to Grumps about her: Was it true? "I'm not a cheetah, I mean, a cheater," Sumac wails. "But I am a liar." Agony to say the word. "I'm really, really sorry, it was a lie not to explain about the game."

"What game?" asks CardaMom.

"It was Blind Man's Buff we were playing, like in Napoleon — olden times. Grumps was blindfolded, see? When he stepped on Oak."

MaxiMum nods, getting it.

"Well. That's a relief," says PopCorn, almost in a whisper.

And it is: Sumac feels so much lighter already, as if she's dropped a heavy bag.

Aspen's accusing stare breaks; she grins. "You're not a cheetah, Sumac, you're a lion."

"Huh?"

"*Lying*, get it? Get it?"

With a great effort, Sumac ignores her sister. She asks the adults, "So he can stay?"

But their long faces tell her she's miscalculated.

"It was an accident," she rushes on, "a total fluke that Oak crawled right under Grumps's boot!" Was this the Lotterys' bad luck that's been waiting for them all these years?

"Still," says MaxiMum, "Iain needs constant, professional supervision so he doesn't hurt himself or anyone else."

"Or wander off again," PapaDum puts in.

"He didn't wander!" The last word comes out in a squeak. "Not like across a train track. He took a taxi to the airport, which is a perfectly sensible thing to do, and he'd have gotten as far as Faro if you meanie pigs hadn't canceled his credit card."

"True," says PopCorn with a sigh. "But my dad needs so much help."

Sumac flails for a second. The dads and moms didn't see Grumps the way she did, all knobbly and out of place against the massive glass wall of the airport. They don't realize that he belongs to the Lotterys now.

Then, noticing that Brian's conked out in the middle of the trampoline, still wearing her fire truck, she thinks of something. "Oak needs help too," she says, "but we're never going to send him away to live with strangers!"

"Eminently logical, as usual," murmurs MaxiMum.

"Oh, come on. . . ." That's PapaDum.

"It's neur, neuro —" Argh, thinks Sumac, what's that word?

"Nureyev? The ballet dancer?" suggests PopCorn, puzzled.

"Brains not being the same as each other," says Sumac, "and that's OK."

"Neurodiversity," supplies MaxiMum, nodding.

"The difference is that we all love Oak," says PapaDum.

"Well, I bet if we practiced a bit more, we could love Grumps," Sumac tells them, looking from face to face. "It's only been three and a half weeks. Surely it'll get easier? Like the elderberries that need cooking before they're friendly to stomachs."

CardaMom reaches out for Sumac's hand.

She scrabbles for a good argument. "It's like your proverb," she tells PapaDum. "We're only halfway up the coconut tree, and there's no point stopping there, because we don't even have half a coconut yet."

"But, Sumac —"

"He's our *plus one*," she roars at them all. "Like it or lump it."

✳

Brian's been watching Grumps with a scowl all week, in case he's going to stamp on Oak again. Finally she announces at dinner, "I don't be hating you now."

An awful silence, and then Grumps says, "Thanks."

"Oak don't be hating you too."

"Glad to hear it." Grumps shakes Oak by the hand (not the one with the taped fingers). Then he does the craziest thing: He folds his huge, brown-blotched, red-veined ear into its hole, holds his nose, and blows, and the ear pops out.

Oak laughs so much his diaper leaks.

Either Grumps is making a mega effort to fit in, Sumac thinks, or his pills are helping to slow down the hole-forming in his brain. CardaMom says maybe the Lotterys are just getting to know the man better. (Like, those stuffed heads on his wall — the wolverine and the caribou and the sheep — it turns out he didn't shoot them at all; he just collected them at yard sales.) Also, the parents are getting the hang of taking turns keeping an eye on Grumps, without him noticing and losing his temper. He even seems to be eating more of PapaDum's *weirdy salads*, but maybe PapaDum's making them a bit less *weirdy* so Grumps will eat them?

Their grandfather comes along to the next Fleeting and puts toilets at the top of the agenda. The Lotterys compromise on a flush-every-time policy, but with a dam installed in each tank to reduce the water used by about a third. (Brian's totally confused now; Sumac thinks her little sister may be flushing before she pees as well as after, and sometimes — judging by startled yelps that are heard from the washroom — during.)

Grumps still spends a lot of the time on his own in his room. (Several Lotterys have offered to paint over the sky and clouds and sun, but he keeps saying not to bother, so Sumac suspects he likes it.) But he's sometimes to be found down in the Orchestra Pit — turns out he can play the piano pretty well — or reading the paper on the Derriere, or even (slowly) walking on the treadmill.

Grumps and Brian keep those marbles she stole from Toytally Awesome in a tin hidden in the Wild so Oak won't swallow them, and they get them out every afternoon when Oak's kaput, to talk very boringly about bosses and puries. Brian seems to be winning all Grumps's puries off him, or maybe he's letting her? Then every evening after dinner, MaxiMum smokes her one cigarette with Grumps, and Wood and Diamond invite him to come check out what's new in the Ravine.

In his poker-faced way, Grumps teases Catalpa about the length of Quinn's hair and whether the boy is actually capable of speaking or was born without a tongue. When Catalpa finally agrees to let her family hear Game of Tones's cover version of "Happy" (which Sic's already tracked down online and pronounced "not as excruciating as you'd expect"), Grumps nods along seriously as if he's listening to Bach.

Sumac hears him remarking to Aspen that she looks the

spit of her grandmother, the first Elspeth. She's about to tell him that Aspen's bios are CardaMom and PapaDum, actually, so Aspen didn't get any of her genes from him or his dead wife . . . and then she decides this is probably another button-your-lip moment.

As for Sumac, she mostly talks books with him — especially old ones. He gets quite excited about her reading *The Princess and the Goblin* because of George MacDonald being Scottish, and all the stuff about mining; it turns out Grumps was a mining engineer for forty years.

All this time he's had the impression that Sumac's about twelve, "but undersized, you know, from the orphanage."

"I wasn't ever in an orphanage, remember?"

"Oh, aye," says Grumps, as if he's doubting Sumac's memory but doesn't want to call her on it.

Anyway, she supposes it's a compliment that he thought she was mature enough to be twelve instead of nine.

❋

On Sunday evening Sumac passes Sic doing up his Day-Glo laces in the Hall of Mirrors and adding "Vrum-vrum with Lin-Lin" to the Where Board.

"Who's Lin-Lin?" she asks.

"It means *beauty of a tinkling bell*," he says with a hollow laugh.

"Mrs. Zhao?"

"Dui," says Sic with a nod, so that must mean yes. "Spotted it on her phone bill." He's set himself a challenge of squeezing the max out of his driving sessions by learning a hundred words in Mandarin. "Beauty of a pounding gong, more like. *Check your mirror!"* He imitates Mrs. Zhao's stern accent. *"Eyes where you wanna go!"*

"Isn't she getting any less bossy, then?"

Sic pats her shoulder. "Adults don't change, kiddo, you just get used to them, figure out some workarounds."

"And is she used to you yet?" Sumac wonders, noticing his socks: one gray Argyle, one Winnie the Pooh.

Her brother grins. "Now she's got her head around my having two moms and two dads, she insists I should obey all of them all the time — like, filial piety times four."

"What's filly —"

"Being nice to your parents. *Work hard, keep family strong!* And she's impressed that we've got Grumps living with us — that's filial piety big-time."

"Is your driving getting any better?" Sumac remembers to ask, when her brother's halfway out the door.

"Buzhidao," says Sic, his hand doing a so-so gesture. "Hard to tell, when she calls me an idiot all the time."

Out in the Wild, the others are waiting for Sumac to lead the Monarch Tag.

A butterfly nerd couple — not two nerdy butterflies, but a human husband and wife who were nerds about butterflies — started the project here in Toronto back in the 1940s. Sunset's the best, when the monarchs are roosting. You creep up from behind and sweep the net over the butterfly, then flip the end of the net over the handle so it can't escape. Hold the edge of the wings through the mesh, reach in with the other hand and grasp it gently by its back. Only the boy ones have a black spot on the hind wing.

"Gotcha," howls Aspen.

Sumac goes over to check. "No, that's a viceroy — see the black line across the hind wings?"

Aspen makes her evilest orc face at Sumac and turns her net inside out to release the viceroy.

Brian spends most of the time chasing them, waving her net and shouting, "Butterfly, stop!" They fly about twenty kilometers an hour, so she has no chance, especially

in her fire truck, but nobody wants to discourage her. Brian's legs are bloody from bramble scratches, but she doesn't even seem to notice.

Kid fingers are actually better at sticking on the tiny tags than adult ones. You note down the tag code, date, location, name, and address on the data sheet, peel the backing off the tag, press it over the mitten-shaped cell on the wing . . . then release the monarch on the nose of whichever kid caught it. That last bit isn't science, just tradition. It feels tickly but amazing: like you're a launchpad for a tiny rocket.

"It's so that somebody might find this butterfly after she's been to Mexico and back and died," Sumac explains to Brian, "and they'll email to say where she ended up."

"I don't want her died!"

"Just of being old," says Sumac, regretting that she mentioned that detail. "She'll be really tired by then."

"Us too?"

"No," Sumac tells her, "next spring we'll still be young."

Aspen says, "Grumps!"

"You mean that he's old?"

"No, I mean, we could tag him in case we lose him again. Maybe an electronic one like the thing on CardaMom's suitcase that beeps if she walks too far away from it."

Sumac frowns. "I don't think Grumps would put up with that. It might feel like he's a dog, or under house arrest."

"It wouldn't give him an electric shock or anything," says Aspen.

"No, but imagine if he's going for a walk and suddenly starts beeping. . . . Awkward!"

They can't find any more monarchs so they head back toward the house. Topaz is splayed in a patch of sun like a furry orange starfish, so Aspen kneels to stroke her belly. In the vegetable patch, PapaDum and Grumps are transplanting shallot seedlings. Watching the two men bent over, working without a word, it occurs to Sumac that PapaDum might suit Grumps as a son better than PopCorn.

Brian wants a snail race, so she and Sumac and Aspen each find one in the bushes and put them down on a shady slab. In chalk they draw one start line and one finish line.

Sumac remembers a joke from the book, exactly the right one for this moment. She takes a breath and remembers not to announce that she's telling a joke. "What does a snail say when it's riding on a turtle's back?"

Aspen looks at her warily.

To deliver the punch line, Sumac makes her best attempt at the facial expression of a joyriding snail. "Wheeeeeeeee!"

Aspen, Brian, PapaDum, and even Grumps burst out laughing.

"You did it," cries Aspen.

Sumac sticks out her tongue and smiles.

"Wheeeee!" repeats Grumps, chuckling.

"Your grandfather's good with a trowel," says PapaDum, straightening up and arching his back till it clicks.

"Dig, dig, dig," Grumps sings under his breath,

And your muscles will grow big.
Don't mind the worms,
Just ignore their squirms . . .

The kids all laugh at that.

"Had a pig club," he adds.

"What did it do?" asks Aspen.

"The pig?"

"No, your club."

Grumps shrugs. "Went round collecting scraps, fed our pig everything we could find. Rabbits too."

"You fed it *rabbits*?" asks Sumac in horror.

"No, you numpty! We kept a few rabbits too, on the side, like."

"You teached them tricks?" Brian wants to know.

He stares at her. "Kids today, no sense of reality. The rabbits were for the pot!" He mimes munching. "But Sausage Day, when the pig got butchered" — he slits his throat with a finger — "that was champion."

Brian's face contorts.

"This was during the war, yeah?" asks PapaDum. "You must have been hungry."

"Not on Sausage Day," says Grumps, stabbing his trowel into the dirt.

✳

Brian insists on wearing her fire truck to *The Wizard of Oz* because it's like a drive-in.

"More like a walk-in," says Sic.

The show's in the park around the corner, with a big white sheet hung over a wall for a screen, starting about 8:20 so the last rays of the sun don't get in the audience's eyes.

PopCorn immediately joins the drumming circle that's formed under the big walnut tree. CardaMom spreads out the black-and-red raven blanket, and PapaDum serves up his homemade mint tea from one big flask and chocolate milk from another. People are buying beers from coolers and cooking hot dogs and skewers over a fire pit. It all smells so good, Sumac feels hungry even though she had curried-salmon-on-a-plank an hour ago. A music video comes on, and kids and some adults are already jumping around.

A guy pushes a cart with *Random Acts of Kindness and Senseless Beauty* painted on the side, handing out slices of watermelon. "Eleven over here," calls Catalpa.

CardaMom makes a slapping gesture at her. "We can share," she tells him.

He's got huge black plugs in his earlobes and a shaved head with two buns on top. "No probs, no sweat, big whoop, eleven it is."

"Actually, sorry, twelve," says Sumac. "We used to be eleven, but now our grandfather lives with us too." Little by little, she supposes, Grumps is going to turn into a Lottery too.

"The full dozen, cool," says the watermelon guy, nodding.

Like eggs, thinks Sumac, or months, or roses.

Now the MGM lion is roaring on the screen and the violins are soaring from the speakers hidden in the bushes. Brian says it's *too louderer*, so Grumps fits his hands over her ears.

Having him at Camelottery is not exactly *cool*, Sumac thinks. More like a complicated cat's cradle that keeps getting snagged till you figure it out. But still, in the end, *big whoop*.

✳

The next morning Brian's fire truck's lost — because she fell asleep before Dorothy even met the Munchkins, and PapaDum carried her home hours later, and each Lottery thought somebody else was in charge of the truck. She's crying her eyes out and asking to go back to the park to check again "in case the robber be sorry and druv it back."

Sic's trying to comfort her with a long yarn about a family of raccoons dragging it behind a bush to raise their seven babies in.

"No use bawling," says Grumps with a snort.

Brian goes puce.

Sumac remembers exactly why she's disliked this old man from day one.

"Plenty more cardboard where that came from," he tells Brian. "What would you say to a Spitfire?"

"What a spitfire?"

Sumac stiffens: Doesn't it mean a girl with a bad temper?

"Only the pride of the Royal Air Force, best single-seater fighter plane ever made," says Grumps.

Brian's eyes light up.

Today's the August full moon, so most of the Lotterys are getting ready for Rakhi. Sumac and Catalpa decorate the special threads for tying on their brothers while PapaDum struggles with the chocolate truffles. He's trying to roll some in cocoa, some in nuts, some in cinnamon, some in coconut, but they keep sticking to his hands because of the heat, and Topaz is twining round his legs mewing for a snack.

"Can I make some?" Aspen wanders in from outside, shiny with sunblock and sweat.

"Which," asks PapaDum, "truffles or Rakhi threads?"

"Both."

"Not at the same time!" they all chime together.

PapaDum straightens up with a grunt. "These need to go back in the refrigerator for a while."

"Then I'll do threads," says Aspen.

"Why not?" Sumac makes herself say it.

But Aspen's mooched off already with a "back in a minute," so that's good; she'll forget all about it.

"Three brothers, multiplied by four sisters," murmurs Catalpa, "that's twelve."

"Actually," says PapaDum, "a woman can tie one around the wrist of any man she considers a sort of brother for life, so your moms could have another four, to tie on me and PopCorn."

"Fine," says Catalpa, "keep us slaving away all day."

Braiding threads, Sumac gazes out the window. Grumps is lifting Brian into the Spitfire they've spent all morning making out of boxes; her little legs thrash with excitement. (Sic is sprawled nearby to keep an eye on them, with that fat book called *Cryptonomicon* he's read so often it's broken in half.) The finishing touch is a propeller — made of wire hangers and packing tape and attached to the nose. Grumps bends and spins it. "What about Grumps?" she asks. "He doesn't have a sister."

"He has two of them, actually, but they live in Glasgow and New Zealand," says PapaDum.

"Let's call him a sort-of-brother too, then," Sumac suggests.

"Six more coming up," says Catalpa, heaving a sigh. But you can tell she's enjoying herself.

So is Sumac. How compatible she and her big sister would be, she thinks — if only they liked each other.

"Ammi," PapaDum's saying to his mother via Skype, "why don't you supervise the girls, so I can get the onion bhaji in the stove and . . . No, I don't fry my bhaji, baking's much healthier."

Sumac can hear Dadi Ji's outraged voice over the top of his.

On the tablet, their grandmother watches Catalpa and Sumac decorate their folded and knotted bundles of silk threads. "Have you put gold threads in with the red and yellow?" she asks, putting her face so near the webcam that she looms. "That's even more auspicious."

Sumac meets Catalpa's eyes. They ran out of gold after the first five.

"A few," Catalpa tells their grandmother. "And lots of beads and sequins."

"When you've braided and tied them, don't forget to fluff the ends with a toothbrush. Now which of you is preparing the special thali plate?"

Catalpa's ready for this one. "We wondered if you'd possibly have time to be in charge of that, Dadi Ji?"

"If you prefer, my dear," says their grandmother, readjusting her pink veil above her little gold glasses.

On the other side of the Mess, PapaDum gives a thumbs-up. Because between the betel leaves, the diya lamp, the roli powder arranged in a swastika (the lucky kind, not the evil Nazi kind), the rice, the incense sticks, and the gods know what else, the Lotterys are likely to get it wrong and deeply offend some deity (e.g., their grandmother).

"Now, you'll give your brothers sweets and put tilak powder on their foreheads, and have they prepared the envelopes of cash?"

"The boys are going to give the girls sweets too," Sumac tells her.

"That's not very traditional," she scolds.

"Well, let's face it, Ammi," PapaDum calls, "nor are we."

A while later, Grumps and Brian stagger into the Mess very red-faced, in need of lemonade.

"Grumps, would it be all right if we tie bracelets on you at the party?" asks Catalpa.

"What party?"

"Rakhi," Sumac reminds him for the third time today, "the only festival in the world that celebrates brothers and sisters."

"Still sounds a bit makey-uppy to me," he mutters, fiddling with his new chunky black watch.

By *makey-uppy* he means Hindu. But Sumac lets it go. "So can we?"

"Couldn't care less, hen."

"It says Tuesday the twentieth of August," says Aspen, reading his watch over his shoulder. "Unfair! I want a watch that tells me all that."

"You have two watches," says Sumac, "but you never remember to put them on."

"You don't even go to school, missy," Grumps says to Aspen, "so what do you care what day it is?"

"You know you don't have to wear that thing?" Catalpa says in his ear.

"It's waterproof," says Grumps. "Kept it on in the shower this morning."

"No, but — it's surveillance," says Catalpa. "Big Brother, watching you by GPS."

"Is there a wee camera?" he asks, peering into the screen.

"I don't mean *actually* watching you, just —"

"If you were gone all day, Iain," PapaDum explains, "we could look up a website to see where you were, that's all."

"Doesn't it bother you that they're infringing your rights?" Catalpa demands.

"Young lady," says Grumps, "you'll find the world is full of things a sight more bothersome than a free watch."

"My friend Liam has a GPS chip in his backpack," says Aspen, "and he totally freaked his folks out by going on a sleepover and accidentally leaving the backpack on the bus so it went around and around the city. . . ."

"What say that?" says Brian, pointing at the word *SOS* on Grumps's watch.

"That's my special button for emergencies," says Grumps, pressing it hard.

"*Wah wah wah wah,*" Brian squeals.

"Hi again, Dad," says PopCorn's voice from the watch — very small and tinny — a second later.

"That you, Reginald?" Grumps lifts his wrist to his mouth.

"Who else do you think would call you *Dad?*"

Grumps nods. "Where are you at the minute?"

"In the basement sorting socks. Do you need something else?"

"Wouldn't say no to a cup of tea."

A squeaking sound that turns out to be PopCorn laughing.

When Isabella comes over, Sumac and she escape all the way up to the top of the house. "Ready?" asks Sumac. "Think ice palace." She throws open the door on which she's hung up her carved *Sumac's Room* sign at last.

"Oo!"

"PopCorn's been slaving over this for the past two days, that's why it's still fumey."

"I adore the smell of paint," says Isabella, sniffing. "*So* classy, two walls white and two silver, and the fairy lights everywhere."

"They're icicles, see?" Sumac shows her their tips.

"Wow! And snowflake curtains," cries Isabella, pointing. "This room's way more grown-up than your old one."

Sumac gazes around. She's never going to do or plan anything babyish or dumb in here.

"Oo, look," says Isabella, face pressed to the window. "Wood's got a giant bow, like Robin Hood."

"Don't get him started on how he carved it himself out of yew," Sumac warns her.

The doorbell, far below. After a few seconds, CardaMom yells, "Somebody get that!"

Sumac notices a quote in PapaDum's neat capitals on a mirror as she hurries downstairs and through the Hall of Mirrors to answer the door:

IF YOU'RE FINISHED CHANGING,
YOU'RE FINISHED.

Underneath someone's added, barely legibly,

All pigs fed and ready to fly.

It's Gram (MaxiMum's mom), who's driven into town with two trays of her tamarind balls — they look like donuts, but they're fruit paste — and a bag of "totally *un*educational toys, heh heh heh," according to Aspen. Who pops a whole tamarind ball into her mouth, then chokes because it's a hot-pepper one.

Dada Ji (recently turned ninety, but the same as ever in his black turban) and Dadi Ji arrive next with one box of lurid orangey-yellow jalebi, and another full of diamonds of cashew-paste barfi, which Sumac enjoys so long as she doesn't think about the name. They're decorated with vark, which is actual silver beaten very thin; you'd think it would poison you, but apparently not.

The shaggy lawn behind Camelottery is filling up. Mrs. Zhao and her silently smiling husband arrive with a huge tureen of chicken feet soup, which gets Gram very excited because she grew up on the stuff in Jamaica.

Brian zooms by, her Spitfire wings poking several guests in the butt. Aspen is showing off Slate's party tricks, and Opal keeps shrieking "Meh!" No sign of the cats: This crowd is too much even for Topaz.

"I heard Mrs. Zhao telling MaxiMum that Sic's a hard worker and will go far," Wood reports.

"No!" says Catalpa. "Don't dare tell him. If that head swells any more, it'll burst."

Quinn gazes at her as if she's the wittiest girl he's ever met as well as the gorgeousest.

"Is Grumps being civil to the guests?" Sumac wonders.

"I heard him make some crack to Jagroop about how he'd thought he wasn't going to have any grandkids, and now he's got them sprouting like weeds," says Wood. "But hey, weeds are just flowers that grow easily."

Sumac notices Grumps is deep in conversation with Gram now, so she sidles up to check he's not calling her *colored* or anything.

"Packed off to Rothesay — that's on an island," he's saying, "with no more than a toothbrush and a clean pair of scants. Exasperated, like."

Gram has her head on one side. "You felt . . . exasperated?"

He shakes his head. "Ejected? No, that's James Bond with his ejector seat."

What's he on about?

"Thousands of us weans were, for fear of the, you know —" He mimes what looks to Sumac like tomatoes dropping and bursting apart. "Mask, tag with my number on it . . . Exiled, is that it?"

PapaDum's parents are hovering on the edge of the conversation. "I must confess to feeling somewhat exiled when we came to Canada too, in 1965," says Dada Ji.

Gram nods. "I had to rush out to buy the children snowsuits."

"No, Canada was later," Grumps corrects them. "I'm talking about when I was a boy, nine years old, got shunted —" A gasp of frustration. "Tip of my tongue. Vacuumed?"

Sumac is still thinking about the exploding tomatoes. A mask, what kind of mask? "In the war?" she guesses.

Grumps turns on her. "Of course, otherwise there'd have been no risk of us getting blown to smithereens!"

There's no use expecting this man to be grateful when you figure out what he means.

"Ah, yes, the Blitz, very good, dear, you know your history," says Dada Ji, nodding at Sumac. "You were evacuated, then, Iain?"

"Evacuated, that's it!" Grumps roars it so loudly that Mrs. Zhao gives him a repressive look from right across the Wild.

Sumac's heard of the Blitz, but she didn't know it happened to Glasgow as well as London. Now she comes to think about it, the whole island of Britain isn't very long; not far for a Spitfire to fly, or whatever the Nazis had. So it's happened to Grumps twice: transported from his real life to a brand-new one, without being consulted. Are we his

Blitz, she wonders. Or maybe dementia's the Blitz, and we're the island he's been evacuated to?

He's talking to Mr. Zhao now, she notices, and rubbing Diamond's head. "Goes better on three legs than most dogs on four," he's saying.

PapaDum rings a special bell, which means it's time for the Rakhi ceremony.

Sic reads aloud from a book of Indian legends about when Shachi tied a thread around her husband Indra's wrist to boost his powers of mind and help him defeat demons. The story sounds a bit like a Marvel comic, but that's probably just the way Sic says it.

"I thought the party was about brothers, not husbands," mutters Aspen in Sumac's ear.

She shrugs, watching Grumps and wondering whether anything could boost his *powers of mind* at this stage. Thinking about her own demons of nastiness and meanness, she tells them: *Begone!*

Oak finds having his Rakhi threads tied on a hoot and keeps hiding his fat wrist behind his back so it takes all the girls and women a while to get it done. Aspen does vicious tickle attacks while tying hers on the boys and men in her family, so that slows things down too.

"May all be happy," Dada Ji recites,

May all be free from ills,
May all behold only the good,
May none be in distress.

At which point, PopCorn starts crying.

Grumps turns his head away, looking mortified.

"You no need to pee now," Brian tells PopCorn.

"That's a relief," he whispers, and blows his nose.

"And then you pray for your brothers' well-being and happiness," Dada Ji tells the women and girls. *"May you be well and happy —"*

"May you be well and happy," they chorus.

Wood and Aspen exchange hideous grimaces from across the grass.

"And then, menfolk, you take this pledge. *I vow to protect my sisters —"*

"I vow to protect my sisters," they chant.

"Protect? Isn't that a bit patronizing?" Catalpa wants to know.

CardaMom claps a hand over her black-lipsticked mouth.

"— and help them to climb over any obstacles —"

"— and help them to climb over any obstacles —"

"Or kick them over," yells Catalpa.

Aspen laughs and does a karate kick, accidentally getting Dadi Ji in the stomach.

There's a last-minute kerfuffle when Brian insists on being a brother and having threads tied on her. But then she wants to tie one on Oak too, because "I be sister *and* brother." Then Aspen remembers that Slate and Opal probably have litter- and hatch-sisters that they miss, though tying bracelets on a rat and a parrot is likely to be a fiddly business. Luckily Sumac has extra Rakhi in her pocket and hands them out to anyone who wants one, because really, who cares so long as the threads get tied.

THE THANK-YOU PAGE

Authors steal ideas all the time. But like the tiny family in Mary Norton's series *The Borrowers*, we prefer to call it borrowing. Here's a grateful shout-out to the folks, young and old, from whom I've borrowed most:

Debra Westgate for professional advice on kids in all their wonderful oddity, and Gráinne Ní Dhúill, Aoife and Fionnuala Westgate for snail races; Astra Vainio-Mattila (reader extraordinaire and member of my first-ever Focus Group); Helen, Asa, and Sophie Thomas, and Julian Patrick for tales of Camp Wanapitei; Tamara Sugunasiri for asking for a book like this (I planned it over the course of one of your great dinners); Derek Scott for Pied Piping, plus Maya Scott (Focus Group member) for teaching yourself to read and shaving your head at three; Laurent Ruffo-Caracchini for making teenage brilliance likable; Tracey "Trace the Ace" Rapos for your ink; my niece and goddaughter, Dearbhaile Ní Dhubhghaill, for your passions for animals and Elvish; our Montreal family (Jeff, Declan, and Loïc Miles, and especially Hélène Roulston for MaxiMal calm); Holly Harkins-Manning and Richard, Owen, Silas, Duncan,

Malcolm, Seamus Finnegan (Focus Group member), and Charlotte Manning, for making more look so much merrier; Alison Lee and Sarah Redekop, especially for brainstorming tree names for the Lotterys on the train to Menton; novelist Amanda Jennings for putting the name of her goddaughter Seren Johnson in this book as a fund-raiser for CLIC Sargent (the UK's leading cancer charity for young people); Sidney and Madeleine Gervais, and thanks so much Kelly Gervais for driving me around Parkdale in search of Camelottery; Ali Dover for sanity-saving hilarity and dispatches from the wilder shores of parenting and woo, plus Zelda Dover for inimitable scowls; my sister-in-law Bernie Donoghue for endless patience; Ashlin Core (Focus Group member) for mismatched socks; Kate Ceberano for your daughter's "imagic that"; Vivien Carrady and Sheldon, Desana, Seth, and Alex Rose for sudden headstands and grace under fire; the Bélanger-Ferrés (Danièle, Stéphane, Loup-Yann, Guillaume, and Tristan), as well as Samantha and Mallory Brennan and Jeff, Gavin, and Miles Fullerton, for showing how families can cherish everyone's talents; Bipasha Baruah, Paul Perret, and Ahaan Perret Baruah for doing it your way; Eric Gansworth, Roberta Duhaime, and Olugbemisola Rhuday-Perkovich for reading the manuscript and giving me the benefit of their kind advice; and Caroline Hadilaksono for the glorious illustrations.

A special thanks to my parents, Frances and Denis Donoghue (who'd have preferred to have two rather than eight, but love us all unflaggingly), and my beloved Chris, Una, and Finn Roulston (Focus Group member) for daily inspiration and laughs.

This book was edited by Arthur Levine and designed by Elizabeth B. Parisi, Abby Denning, and Caroline Hadilaksono. The text was set in Adobe Caslon Pro, a typeface designed by Carol Twombly based on pages printed by William Caslon, with hand-lettering by Caroline Hadilaksono. The display type was set in Jande Safe and Sound, Beloved Sans. The book was printed and bound by LSC Communications in Harrisonburg, Virginia. Production was supervised by Rebekah Wallin, and manufacturing was supervised by Angelique Browne.